REALLY
Raoulino

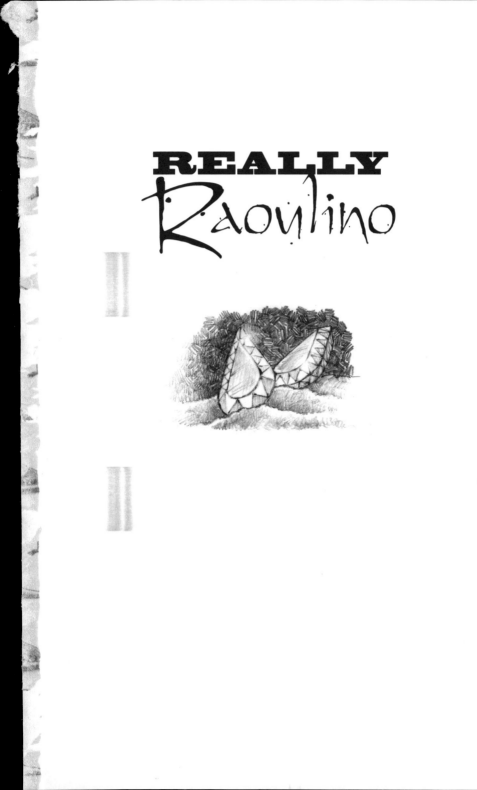

Text copyright © 2006 by Dina Fischbein
Illustrations copyright © 2006 by Bill Crews
All rights reserved
CIP data is available

Published in the United States in 2006 by Handprint Books
413 Sixth Avenue
Brooklyn, New York 11215
www.handprintbooks.com

Book design by Irene Vallye

First Edition
Printed in China
ISBN: 1-59354-151-1
2 4 6 8 10 9 7 5 3 1

REALLY Raoulino

DINA FISCHBEIN
ILLUSTRATIONS BY BILL CREWS

Handprint Books Brooklyn, New York

To my family and my friends, with love—

D.F.

To my mother, Ellie, and father, Chris,

for their lifelong support, encouragement, and love

that fed me in the pursuit of my passion—

B.C.

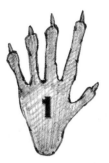

When they brought Raoulino to the Metropolitan Zoo, the scientists were very excited. All day long, important professors studied him from the tip of his nose to the end of his long green tail.

"Definitely a lizard," said one professor.

"Definitely not," said another.

"Well, he's certainly a reptile of some sort," said a third professor.

"We can't be certain of that," said a fourth professor.

They argued for nearly an hour. Finally, they put a large sign on Raoulino's cage which said,

REPTILIA?

INCOGNITUM INCOGNITA

(which is a scientific way of saying, "Maybe it's a reptile, but we're not really sure what it is."). Then they turned off the lights and left.

It was very dark in the reptile house. Raoulino lay on the floor of his cage, trembling. All around him he could hear breathings and rustlings from the other cages. Green and yellow eyes stared at him through the blackness.

"Hey, what are you anyway?" whispered a voice.

But Raoulino didn't answer. Exhausted by his long, hard day, he curled up into a ball and fell asleep without saying a word.

The next morning, Raoulino awoke very early. Bright sunlight streamed through the narrow windows high up on the walls of the reptile house. Raoulino saw that he was in a clean little cage made of wire mesh. There was soft sand on the floor, some pretty green plants in one corner, and a round dish full of water in another. Raoulino walked over to the dish, took a big drink, and peeked into the cage next to his.

His heart almost stopped beating. Right in the center, coiled up and snoring peacefully, was a black and white cobra!

Raoulino was terrified.

Holding his breath so he wouldn't make a sound, he backed away, trying to get as far from the large snake as he could. He had almost made it to the far side of his cage when he heard a loud splash and a sudden burst of raucous laughter. Whirling around, Raoulino saw a round, green pool filled with alligators at the other end of the room. The huge animals lifted their heads out of the water and grinned at him wickedly.

"Oh," wailed Raoulino. "I don't like it here! I want to go home!"

He threw himself against the front of his cage, but the walls didn't budge. He tried to bite his way out, but the wire was much too tough for his little teeth.

"Hey, calm down," said a gentle voice from the cage on his left. "It's all right. No one's going to hurt you, I promise."

Raoulino stopped biting at the cage and turned around. In the cage on his left was a small, slender brown lizard with five white stripes running along his body and a bright blue tail.

"You'll be fine here," the lizard said gently. "The people take very good care of us. You'll always be safe and warm, and there's plenty of good food.

And all the other animals will be your friends. You'll see."

Raoulino took a deep breath.

"That cobra and those alligators will be my friends?" he asked, in a shaky little voice.

The lizard nodded.

"They will," he said. "And so will I. My name is Basil, by the way. What's yours?"

"My name is Raoulino."

Basil smiled. "Well, it's nice to meet you, Raoulino," he said. "You've certainly put the scientists into a tizzy. They've never seen anything like you before. And neither have I. What kind of animal are you?"

Raoulino sighed. "I don't really know," he said sadly.

Basil looked at him in surprise. "You don't?"

Raoulino shook his head.

"My mother and father and my brothers and sisters are all beautiful green lizards," he said. "But my mother found me in the jungle and brought me home while I was still an egg. We don't know what I am."

"I see," said Basil thoughtfully. "What kind of an egg was it?"

"My mother said it was very special," Raoulino

said eagerly. "It was silvery green, and it glowed like moonlight."

"That's very interesting," said Basil. "The eggs I've read about...."

"Can you really read?" asked Raoulino, with surprise. "I've never heard of an animal that could read!"

"Oh, yes," said Basil. "Mother sent us all to school. It was just a little country place, under a big, flat rock near a stream in Maine, but we had reading and math. Even foreign languages."

"You mean you can speak another language?" asked Raoulino.

"Bird," said Basil.

"Excuse me?"

"I speak Bird," said Basil. "Some days my friend Samantha comes by to chat. She's a sparrow. She tells me all about life in the city outside the zoo."

"Yeah, you should hear it," said a loud, bullying

voice from the opposite row of cages. "A lizard going *tweet, peep, cheep*! You could bust your sides laughing."

"That's Wally, the chuckwalla," said Basil. "Don't mind him."

Raoulino looked across the aisle and saw a tough-looking pink and black lizard with strong, sharp claws. His whole body glittered, as if it were made out of beads.

Wally looked at Raoulino.

"I never heard of no silvery green eggs," he said. "I bet you made that whole thing up!"

"I did not!" Raoulino said fiercely. "I did not!"

"You did, too," shouted Wally.

"Did not!"

"Did, too!"

"Stop this noise at once," said a voice with a hiss.

"Who's that?" whispered Raoulino.

"It's the cobra," said Basil worriedly. "You woke him up."

Raoulino turned and saw that the black and white cobra was now awake. His head was raised, and his tongue flicked in and out angrily.

"I was sleeping," the snake said. "You woke me

with your ridiculous quarrel. Now, what is this all about? Wally?"

"Well, sir," said Wally. "There's a new animal here that says he doesn't know what he is. I was just teasing him a little."

"Wally," said the snake severely, "I have spoken to you many times about upsetting the other animals. Now apologize to the new animal at once."

Wally's head drooped, and he switched his tail back and forth in an embarrassed way.

"I'm sorry, Raoulino," he mumbled. "I didn't mean to hurt your feelings." He raised his head and smiled shyly. "Sometimes I just can't help starting trouble. But I don't really mean what I say."

Raoulino smiled back.

"That's okay, Wally," he said.

"Good," said the cobra. He turned to Raoulino and studied him with his great golden eyes.

"Is it true that you don't know what kind of animal you are?" he asked kindly.

"It's true, sir," Raoulino said. "My mother found me in the jungle and brought me home when I was just a silvery green egg. Nobody knows what I am."

The cobra looked at him carefully. "Well," he said, after a moment, "you're a fine looking animal, whatever you are. Where is your home?"

"Oh, I lived on a wonderful little island," Raoulino said, his voice beginning to quiver. "There were trees and flowers everywhere, and my brothers and sisters and I played together all day long. But one day, when we were playing hide-and-seek, and I was hiding under a banana tree, a man caught me in a net and . . . and. . . ."

A big, hard lump rose in Raoulino's throat, and he couldn't say another word.

"It's all right," said the cobra. "We understand."

"Yeah, I was caught in a net, too," said Wally in his gruff voice. "I felt pretty sad when they first brought me here, but I got used to it."

"We all did," said Basil gently, "and you will, too."

Raoulino's new friends were looking at him so kindly that he began to feel a bit better.

"Well, I guess. . . ." Raoulino began.

He was interrupted by a clang as the iron door of the reptile house opened. A cart full of metal dishes was clattering up the aisle, pushed by a freckle-faced young woman whose hair was as red as a ginger flower. Little sparkly things hung from her ears, swinging and twinkling as she walked. Raoulino was astonished.

"Look at that hair!" he exclaimed. "I never saw a person who looked like that before!"

"Oh, you'll see all kinds of unusual creatures in the zoo," said Basil. "That's Eileen. She's one of the keepers. She's the nicest one."

Raoulino kept staring as Eileen opened his cage, put a fresh piece of newspaper in an empty corner, and placed a dish filled with water and another dish filled with green leaves on top of the paper.

"Try not to knock your dishes over, little fellow," she said. "When we get the money for the new reptile house, we'll be able to buy plenty of clean sand. But for now, we have to do the best we can."

She patted Raoulino gently on the back, locked the cage again, and moved down the aisle.

Raoulino was hungry. He looked at the pile of strange green leaves in his dish.

"What are these things?" he asked Basil.

Basil peered through the wire at Raoulino's dish.

"Lettuce and dandelion greens. Go ahead and try some. They look good."

Raoulino took a tiny bite of leaf and began to chew. Basil was right. They were good. Really fresh and juicy. He was just about to take another mouthful when the iron door clanged again. Then he heard a low murmur, like the sound of the sea on the shore.

Raoulino raised his head.

"What's that sound?" he asked Basil.

Basil looked up from his dish.

"Oh, that's the people," he said. "They come every day. It's fun to watch them. There are so many different kinds."

The people flowed past Raoulino's cage while he ate his breakfast. Raoulino was amazed at how many different sizes, shapes, and colors they were. Most of them looked at him quietly for a few moments and moved on, but one little boy scratched his fingers across the front of Raoulino's cage and yelled, "Hey, turn around, stupid lizard."

Immediately, Eileen rushed over, spoke sharply to the boy, and sent him away.

"I'm sorry about that, little guy," she said to Raoulino. "When we get the new reptile house, the cages will be made of soundproof glass, and that won't happen anymore."

The people kept coming all day. Many of them stood together in small groups, the big ones carrying little ones in their arms or holding them by the hand. Raoulino felt sure they were families. A painful lump formed in Raoulino's throat as he watched them.

"Basil," he said, his lips trembling, "don't you miss your family?"

Basil sighed. "Of course I do," he said. "But you must try not to miss them too much."

"Why?" asked Raoulino.

"Well, if you miss them too much, you'll just get sadder and sadder. And that's not good for you."

Raoulino glanced at the end of the opposite row of cages, where a bunch of brightly colored frogs was getting ready for the night, a few of them still giggling and jumping over one another's backs.

"They don't seem to miss their families," Raoulino said.

"They *are* a family," said Basil. "They were hatched here, as many of the animals were, and they've never seen the outside world, so they don't miss it. But animals like us, who've left our families behind . . . we must try hard not to think about them."

"But I *want* to think about them!" Raoulino shouted. "I don't want to forget about my family!"

"Of course you don't," said Basil, with his gentle smile. "Just try not to think about them *all* the time. Okay?"

Raoulino nodded. "Okay," he whispered. "I'll try."

"Good," said Basil. "Now go to sleep. I'll see you in the morning."

The lights in the reptile house grew dim. Raoulino curled up near the leaves in his cage and tried to go to sleep. He thought about his kind green mother and his strong green father and his cute little brothers and sisters. He missed them so much, his heart felt as if it would burst. Two big tears fell from his eyes.

"There's got to be a way to get back home again," he said to himself softly, as his eyes gently closed. "And I'm going to find it! I will . . . I will . . . I will."

Just before he fell asleep, he thought he heard a mean little laugh.

"No," said a squeaky voice, "you won't!"

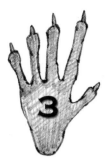

All night long, Raoulino dreamed that he was back home in the jungle with his family. When he awoke the next morning, he felt even sadder than he had the night before.

He rubbed his eyes and stood up to get a drink from his water dish.

I'm so far from home, he thought miserably. *How will I ever get back?*

He took a step toward his dish, glanced down at his feet, and gasped.

Right in front of him, twinkling brightly in the sand, were two beautiful green jewels.

"My goodness!" Raoulino exclaimed.

He looked curiously at the two stones, which glittered like small green stars in the morning light.

"How did they get here?" he asked himself. "Did they fall off Eileen's ears?"

He put his head down and looked at the stones more carefully.

No, he thought. *They're bigger and much brighter than the ones she had.*

He put out his right front leg and touched one gently. It was surprisingly warm. He touched the other one, and it was warm as well. Suddenly, the warmth from the stones seemed to flow through his whole body. Raoulino felt his heart growing lighter. His spirits began to rise.

"Everything's going to be all right," he said to himself firmly. "If I keep on thinking and hoping, I'll come up with a way to get back home. Everything's going to be just fine!"

He looked down at the stones, which were twinkling even more brightly than before.

These are very special stones, Raoulino thought. *I can't let anyone take them away from me!*

Quickly, he pushed them over to the corner of his cage. As fast as he could, he dug a hole under the plants and dropped the stones inside. Then he filled the hole again, smoothing the sand above it until all traces of his digging disappeared.

"Hey, Raoulino," called Wally. "What're ya doing?"

"Uh . . . nothing," Raoulino stammered. "I was just . . . uh . . . tidying up a little."

There was a sudden chirp, a flutter of wings, and a small sparrow with bright black eyes landed on the windowsill.

"Oh! Sam's here!" said Basil happily.

Wally rolled his eyes as Basil rushed to the back of his cage and began to chirp and twitter. The sparrow replied eagerly.

"What is she saying?" asked Raoulino.

"She's telling me the news," Basil said. "The sparrows know everything, because they fly all over the city. Somebody tore out some of the benches in the playground, and there was a fire near the harbor."

Raoulino frowned. "The city sounds like a terrible place," he said.

"It's not so bad," said Basil. "Sam told me there are big parks full of trees and flowers, too."

Basil went back to his conversation, and Raoulino was quiet for a while, trying to imagine the strange city that lay on the other side of the window. Soon, the sky turned cloudy, and a light

rain began to fall. Basil
and Sam finished talk-
ing, and the sparrow
flew away. The iron
door clanged, and the
cart rattled up the aisle
as Eileen brought their

breakfasts and fresh sheets of newspaper. As
soon as she put down the dishes, the animals
began eating.

Basil finished his breakfast quickly. Raoulino
watched as Basil pushed his dish away, put his head
down close to the newspaper, and began slowly
walking back and forth.

"What are you doing?" Raoulino called.

"I'm reading the news," Basil called back.

Raoulino walked over to the mesh wall that
separated his cage from Basil's and looked down at
Basil's paper. All the strange little black marks
looked very confusing.

"Is it hard to read?" he asked shyly.

Basil looked up. "Not really," he said kindly.
"I'll show you."

He dipped his tail into the sand and drew a
curving line. "Now that's an s," he said.

"Oh," said Raoulino. "I thought it was a snake."

"It looks like a snake," said Basil, "but it's the letter *s*. It makes the sound *sssssssssssss*."

"Just like a snake," said Raoulino happily.

Basil smiled at him.

"Right," he said. "Just like a snake. And this is an *o*. The sound it makes is just like its name. If you put the *s* and the *o* together, they make the word *so*."

Raoulino looked at the word.

"So, so, so!" he said loudly. He turned to Basil. "Hey! I can read!"

Basil laughed. "Well, there's a bit more to it than that." He smoothed the sand, dipped his tail into it again, and wrote, 'Raoulino.' "That's your name," he said.

Raoulino looked at it in delight. "What a beautiful long word!" he cried.

Suddenly he heard a bellow so loud, it shook the reptile house.

"What's that?" asked Raoulino.

"It's the alligators," Basil shouted over the noise. "They're having an argument. They don't really hurt each other. They just make a lot of noise and splash water. It doesn't bother Eileen, but it makes Stanley, the other keeper, so upset he gives them extra food to keep them quiet. Look! Here he comes now!"

Raoulino saw a pale young man in green coveralls running down the center of the room. He was shouting angrily, and carrying a big pail. He rushed up to the alligator pool and began flinging handfuls of food at the alligators, who bellowed and splashed a bit longer, then settled down quietly and began to eat. Stanley walked away, muttering to himself and carrying the empty pail.

"He certainly looked upset," said Raoulino.

"He doesn't like reptiles," said Basil. "He used to work in the bird house, and I think we make him nervous. Whenever he picks me up, his hands are always cold and clammy. I hate that."

"Many people dislike us," the cobra said. "They know some of us are dangerous to them, but they cannot tell which. So they hate us all."

"The cobra knows everything," Wally said proudly.

The cobra smiled.

"None of us knows everything, Wally," he said. "But it is true that we cobras are very wise."

Raoulino heard a low murmuring sound as people began to fill the room. He moved to the front of his cage so he could get a good look at them. A group of excited children, led by a pretty young teacher, stopped in front of him. The children stared at Raoulino curiously. Then they sat down on the floor, pulled out pads of paper from their backpacks, and started to write.

"What are they doing?" Raoulino whispered to Basil.

Basil glanced down at one child's book.

"They're drawing pictures of you," he whispered back.

"Really?" said Raoulino. Feeling rather pleased, he lifted his head, gave the children his best smile, and stood absolutely still while they worked.

When the children finished their drawings, they held them up for their teacher to see, and Raoulino was quite surprised to see that in some of them he looked gray and very long and skinny, and in others he looked green and quite round and fat. One child had even given him six legs!

People are certainly very strange, Raoulino thought to himself.

Raoulino watched the people all day. By late afternoon the crowd had gone, and there was only one visitor left. He was a small, brown-skinned man dressed in a spotless white suit. There was a little white hat on his head. He moved slowly around the reptile house, looking at every animal. When he got to Raoulino's cage he gasped with surprise, and his brown eyes opened wide.

"What are *you* doing here, little fellow?" he said. "I didn't expect to see a creature like *you* in the zoo!"

Raoulino crept closer to the front of his cage and looked curiously at the little man.

"I think he's from my home island," Raoulino said, turning to Basil. "He looks like the people there, and he talks like them, too."

"He's a sailor," Basil said. "The writing on his hat tells the name of the ship. It's the SS *Thomas*."

The sailor smiled at Raoulino. His brown eyes were very kind.

"You're a long way from home, little fellow," he said. "I bet you're homesick, like me."

Eileen, her red curls bouncing, came up to the sailor and tapped him on the shoulder.

"I'm sorry, sir," she said. "The zoo is closing. You'll have to go."

The sailor waved to Raoulino. "Good-bye," he said. "I will come to see you when I can."

Raoulino waved his tail. The little sailor smiled and waved again before he turned away.

"Did you see how happy that sailor was to see me?" Raoulino said as the little man walked away. "He really likes me, I could tell."

He turned to Basil, his eyes bright with hope.

"Do you think he could take me home? All he would have to do is cut the screen on my cage and carry me to his ship!"

"He can't do that," said Basil gently. "That would be stealing. It's against the law."

"But it wouldn't be stealing if I got out of my cage and found his ship myself," said Raoulino.

"No, I guess it wouldn't," said Basil. "But I don't know how you can do that."

"I don't, either," said Raoulino. "Not yet. But if I got to his ship, I'm sure he would take me home. And, some day, I'm going to get to that ship!"

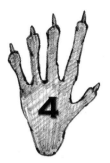

All that night Raoulino lay awake on the sand close to his buried stones and thought about sailing home on the SS *Thomas*.

"Basil," he asked, as soon as his friend woke up the next morning, "where do sailors keep their ships?"

"The ships dock in the harbor," Basil said, yawning. "Sam told me it's west of the zoo."

"Could I walk there?" Raoulino asked.

Basil yawned again. "I suppose you could. But it's pretty far. And it would be very dangerous."

"Dangerous? Why?" asked Raoulino.

"Well, there's the traffic for one thing," said Basil.

"Traffic?" asked Raoulino. "What's that?"

"You know," said Basil. "Cars, buses, trucks. You could easily get run over. And there are dangerous animals, too. Cats. Dogs. Even rats."

"Rats?" said Raoulino with a shudder.

"Lots of them, I'm afraid," Basil said.

Raoulino sat quietly and thought about rats. He was not a fighting animal. His mother and father had taught him to jump onto a leaf and stay there without moving a muscle if he was ever in danger. But what if there were no leaves in the city? What could he do then?

"Basil . . ." he began.

Before he could finish his sentence something went *pop*, and a blinding light flashed in Raoulino's face.

"Basil!" Raoulino shouted as colored circles danced before his eyes. "What was that?"

"Don't worry," Basil said. "It's just a camera. Eileen took your picture. I guess you're kind of famous because nobody knows what you are."

"That's a pretty stupid reason to be famous," said the mean, squeaky little voice Raoulino had heard the other night. "*I* wouldn't want to be famous because of *that.*"

The voice seemed to be coming from the cage above Wally's, but there was no animal in it. When Raoulino looked up, he saw only sand, a water dish, and a big, leafy branch.

"Who said that?" Raoulino asked.

Basil chuckled. "Oh, that's Leon, the chameleon. You have to look very carefully to see him, because he changes color to match whatever he's sitting on."

Raoulino squinted at Leon's cage. At first he couldn't see anything at all. Then, slowly, he made out a pair of round brown eyes, with a sharp little horn over each one. Raoulino stared harder and saw the rest of Leon. He was a small, plump green lizard with a horn over his nose, too, and a very grouchy expression on his face.

Leon gave Raoulino an angry look and very, very

slowly climbed down from his branch. As soon as his feet touched the sand, his green color began to fade, and his plump little body started turning a soft golden brown.

"Wow!" exclaimed Raoulino. "How do you do that?"

"That's *my* secret," squeaked Leon, putting his nose in the air. "And I'm not telling."

"It isn't *your* secret, Leon," Wally jeered. "Any chameleon can do it."

"So what?" Leon squeaked. "I'm a much more interesting animal than Raoulino is. Why don't people stop to look at *me*? Why don't they take *my* picture?"

"Leon," said Basil patiently, "I've told you this before. When people can't see you, they think your cage is empty. If you would move around and change color, plenty of people would look at you."

"I don't *like* to move around," Leon said stubbornly. "Why can't the people just look a little harder?"

Basil shook his head. "Sometimes we have to do things a bit differently, Leon, if we want to make things go our way."

"Well, I'm not doing *anything* differently!"

said Leon with an angry sniff. He finished turning brown, closed his eyes, and seemed to completely disappear.

"He'll figure it out someday," Basil said, chuckling softly.

Raoulino didn't answer. He was pacing back and forth across his cage, thinking furiously. *Maybe I could do things differently, so I wouldn't have to be afraid of rats*, he thought. *But what could I do?*

He paced back and forth a few more times, his legs moving faster and faster each time he crossed his cage.

Then he stopped so suddenly that he sent a spray of sand through the wire mesh, just missing Basil's face.

"I can do *this*!" he shouted happily. "I can exercise and make myself strong enough to fight back if somebody threatens me!"

Immediately, he squatted in place and did twenty-five push-ups. After that, he did twenty-five tail curls. Next, he began jogging around his cage.

"Raoulino," called Basil. "Have you gone crazy? What are you doing?"

"I'm working out," Raoulino panted, "so I can be strong enough to fight a rat."

He finished his last lap, collapsed beside his water dish, and took a long drink.

"Basil," he said, wiping the water from his face with his front leg, "don't you want to go home?"

Basil sighed. "Of course I do," he said. "I would love to see my family again. But it isn't possible. And it's no good wishing for impossible things."

"It's *not* impossible," Raoulino said, his eyes hining. "Are there a lot of ships in the harbor?"

"Raoulino, this is silly. . . ." Basil began.

"No, it's not." Raoulino was hopping up and down with excitement. "How many ships do you think there are?"

Basil shrugged. "I don't know. Sam told me there're lots of everything in the city. People. Buses. Trucks. There are probably a lot of ships, too."

"We can ask Sam to fly to the harbor and look! And if there *are* a lot of ships, she could show us how to get there! Then I could find the SS *Thomas*, and you could find a ship that sails to your home!"

"Ah, if only such a thing could really happen," said the cobra, who was coiled up in his cage listening to their conversation. "How I would love to see my family again. But it would be most difficult to find the harbor. And even if we got there, how could we tell which ships would take us home?"

The animals were silent for a moment, all of them lost in thought. Suddenly, Basil looked up.

"The signs under all our cages have little pictures of our country's flag on them," he said slowly. "It wouldn't be hard to find the ship that's flying the right flag. . . ."

He smiled, and his voice grew hushed and dreamy. "I remember there was a big fleet of red fishing boats that sailed from my town in Maine. They were so pretty . . . I used to watch them from the top of our hill. . . . they belonged to the Portland Fishing Company, and they all had a picture of a silver swordfish on the bow. Maybe . . . maybe I could find one of those."

The cobra's golden eyes flashed brightly for a moment. Then they dimmed.

"First we must escape from our cages," he said with a sigh. "And I've never heard of an animal that has done that."

Raoulino and his friends looked at their cages. Their spirits fell as they studied the heavy metal frames, the thick mesh, the locks.

"We'll *never* get out of here," said Basil, his shoulders drooping.

"We mustn't give up hope," the cobra said, his eyes gleaming once again. "Many things that once seemed impossible have been accomplished. Perhaps we will find a way to do this, too!"

Raoulino stretched out on the sand close to his special stones.

"We will," he said happily. "I'm sure of it. We will!"

There was a clattering sound, and Eileen came up the aisle pushing the breakfast cart. When she got to Raoulino's cage, she smiled and held up a little bowl.

"I brought you a special treat today," she said. "Something you're really going to like. Orchid petals and bougainvillea leaves, all the way from your home island!"

She put the bowl down at the front of Raoulino's cage. A wonderfully sweet fragrance filled the air. Raoulino walked over and sniffed at the leaves and petals.

"They must be from the other side of my island," he said to himself. "I've never seen them before."

Raoulino bent his head and took a little bite of purple petal.

Oh, this tastes so good, he thought happily. He waved his tail at Eileen to say "Thank you," and kept on chewing.

"Enjoy yourself, little guy," she said. "I'll bring you some more of that when I can."

Eileen relocked the door and went away. Raoulino ate every bit of his treat, licking the bowl four times to get every scrap. Just as he finished, the iron door clanged. Visitors began streaming into the reptile house, but Raoulino didn't even look at them. All day long he worked on his exercises so he would be strong when the time came to escape. When the day ended, he was so tired he fell asleep even before the lights were turned out.

Toward morning, Raoulino began to dream. He dreamed he was flying through the air. Below him was a huge gray ocean, and on the ocean there was a white ship. As Raoulino flew closer to the ship, he saw it was the SS *Thomas*. The sailor was standing on the deck calling, "Raoulino! Wake up!"

"Raoulino! Wake up!"

Raoulino opened his eyes. The sun was just beginning to rise. Pale gray light showed at the narrow windows.

"Raoulino! What happened to you?" yelled Wally.

Raoulino blinked his eyes and stood up.

"What are you shouting about, Wally?" he said.

"Look at yourself, Raoulino!" Wally shouted. "You're a different color!"

Raoulino looked down at his legs. Wally was right! His legs, which had been the same dull greenish gray as the rest of him, were now a beautiful, silvery green. He rushed over to his water dish and stared at his reflection. His face was silvery green, too! In fact, all of him was covered with silvery green, eight-sided scales. And wherever a faint ray of sunlight touched him, he glowed!

"I don't believe this," he gasped.

"What's going on?" asked Basil sleepily. He sat up in his cage and rubbed his eyes. When he saw Raoulino, his face grew pale with shock.

"Raoulino!" he called. "What happened to you? Are you all right?"

Raoulino was still staring at his reflection in the water. His heart was beating so fast he could hardly breathe.

"I'm fine," he said. "I don't know what happened, but I feel fine!"

There was so much commotion that Leon actually climbed down from his branch and moved to the front of his cage.

"Oh, great," he grumbled when he saw Raoulino. "Now even *more* people are going to look at him."

Leon was right. When Stanley unlocked Raoulino's cage and saw his new color, he dropped Raoulino's breakfast on the floor and raced out the door. A few minutes later a whole group of people in white coats trooped into the reptile house.

All morning long, they studied Raoulino through their magnifying glasses. They turned him upside down and right side up again, and looked at every inch of him twice. They weighed him and measured him and shone bright lights in his eyes. They frowned and grumbled and mumbled. But they still couldn't figure out what he was.

Word of Raoulino's strange transformation spread quickly throughout the zoo. So many visitors came to see him, and so many cameras flashed in his face, that Raoulino finally hid behind the plants in his cage, and Stanley had to put up a sign that said PHOTOGRAPHS FORBIDDEN!

By the end of the afternoon, Raoulino was so exhausted that he lay down in his special place and shut his eyes. Suddenly, a high, clear voice called, "Look! It's a dragon!"

Raoulino opened his eyes and saw a curly haired little girl standing in front of him. She had a pale, freckled little face, and bright brown eyes. A huge pair of glasses was perched on her little nose. She was carrying a big, fat book with a picture of a dragon on the front.

"Look! It's a little dragon, Mom," she said excitedly, pressing her face to the front of Raoulino's cage. "It says so right here in my book!"

"Emily," said a tall woman who had the same kind of freckles and curly hair as the little girl, "you know very well there are no such things as dragons!"

"But in the book. . . ." Emily began.

"Emily," said her mother, "that book is fiction. Fiction means that what it says is not real."

"But this *is* real!" said Emily. "Listen!" She flipped the open the book and began to read.

"'Young tropical dragons are usually the size of a kitten. Their bodies are silvery green in color, and covered with eight-sided scales that give off a faint glow in sunlight or moonlight. The pupils of their eyes are shaped like black diamonds.'"

"Emily, close that book right now!" said her mother. She turned to the older woman standing beside her and said, "Emily is very bright, of course, but she has *such* an imagination."

"Look at him, Mom," Emily begged. "He *is* about the size of a kitten. He *does* have silvery green, eight-sided scales, and the pupils of his eyes *do* look like black diamonds!"

"If you don't stop making such a fuss, Emily, I'm going to take that book away. All this talk about dragons isn't healthy. Dragons are NOT REAL!"

She took Emily firmly by the hand and marched her out of the reptile house.

"Did you hear that?" Basil said, chuckling. "That little girl thought you were a dragon!"

Raoulino shook his head. "That's ridiculous. A dragon can fly and breathe fire, and I can't do that! Besides, everyone knows there aren't any dragons."

"I liked to hear stories about them when I was little, though," Basil said.

"So did I," said Raoulino. "My mother used to tell them to me before bedtime. She even told me that her grandmother said that dragons live at the top of the tallest mountain on our island."

"Do you think that's true?" Basil asked.

Raoulino shook his head. "No. I think it's just a story. And even if dragons did live there a long time ago, there aren't any now. They're extinct."

"Their eggs stink?" said Wally. "If you've never even seen one, how do you know their eggs stink?"

"I didn't say their 'eggs stink,'" said Raoulino gently. "I said they're *extinct*. That means there aren't any left, not anywhere in the world."

"Oh," said Wally. "I knew that."

Raoulino smiled at Wally and rested his head on his front legs.

"Raoulino," asked Basil in a soft voice, "do you ever think about your other family?"

"What other family?" asked Raoulino sleepily.

"Well, you have the family that brought you up. But you must have another mother somewhere, the one who laid your egg. And maybe you have a father and other brothers and sisters who look just like you. Do you ever think about them?"

"Not really," Raoulino said, yawning. "I have a wonderful family that loves me. And nobody needs more than one family."

"That's true," said Basil.

He yawned, too, and settled down in his cage.

"Good night, Raoulino," he said.

39

"G'night," said Wally.

"Good night," said Raoulino. "See you tomorrow."

Raoulino stretched out comfortably and closed his eyes. For a moment he tried to imagine a silvery green mother and father and brothers and sisters who looked just like him. But just thinking made him feel all confused and dizzy inside. He closed his eyes and slept.

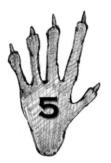

Months went by. The excitement over Raoulino's color change died down, and the days passed peacefully. Now and then, when things got too quiet, the alligators held a little riot.

"Just a little friendly shoving and splashing," they said. "Just to liven things up."

Eileen knew they were only playing and she didn't pay any attention to them, but Stanley always got angry.

Every day, Raoulino did his exercises. He could do a hundred push-ups and tail curls now, without even getting out of breath. He worked hard on his reading, too. First he learned little words, like *an* and *if* and *so*. Next, he learned bigger words, like *police* and *firefighter*. Soon he was able to read really big words, like *government* and *metropolitan*, and kindhearted Basil spent hours telling Raoulino what the words meant. After a few months Raoulino could read almost every word on his newspaper page. He felt very, very smart. But he still couldn't think of a way to escape from the zoo.

One beautiful May morning as he was reading his paper, he saw a headline that said MASTER MAGICIAN REVEALS HIS SECRETS!

Hmm, thought Raoulino, *I wonder what his secrets are*!

He began to read.

MASTER MAGICIAN REVEALS HIS SECRETS!

Mr. Aldo Bandini, the greatest magician of the century, gave his final performance last night. When this reporter asked him for the secret of his great success, Mr. Baldini replied, "Misdirection! Whenever I had to do something tricky onstage, I always did something special with one hand, like waving a big, colorful scarf or a bright light. Then, while my audience was watching that hand, I did what I needed to do with the other. If you don't want people to see what you're doing, you must make sure they're watching something else!"

Raoulino stared thoughtfully at the paper for a few moments. Then he shouted "YES!" at the top of his voice and began leaping joyfully around his cage.

"Raoulino!" exclaimed Basil. "What's the matter with you?"

"I've figured it out!" Raoulino shouted. "I know how we can escape from the zoo. We'll use misdirection!"

"Raoulino," said Basil, "what are you talking about?"

"It's easy," Raoulino said. "You know how crazy Stanley gets when the alligators riot. Well, on a day when he brings our breakfasts, we'll ask the alligators to make a lot of noise at the exact moment that he opens each one of our cages. He'll get distracted and run out to get their extra food, and he'll forget to lock our cages. Then we can jump out and escape through the front door! We'll be free!"

Basil's eyes opened wide.

"You know," he said thoughtfully, "it could work. It really could!"

His bright blue tail began to tremble with excitement.

"Sam can study the signs under our cages to learn what the flags of our countries look like,"

Basil said. "Then she can check the harbor every day and tell us when ships flying our flags are docked there. Maybe the SS *Thomas* will be there, and Raoulino can go home with his sailor friend! And she can look for a Portland Fishing Company boat for me. If we ask her, I'm sure she'll show us the way to the harbor, too!"

"Will she really do all that?" asked Raoulino.

"Of course she will," Basil said. "She's a good friend."

"I will ask the alligators to help us," the cobra said. "Trident, their leader, and I are old friends. I am sure he will do his best!"

"This is a really stupid idea," squeaked Leon. "What if you travel all that way and find your homes are gone? Did you ever think of that?"

"What are talking about, Leon?" said Raoulino impatiently. "Of course our homes are still there."

"Mine isn't," said Leon, his lower lip quivering. "People riding on big machines came and knocked down my whole forest. If the zoo people hadn't brought me here, I don't know what would have happened to me. There was no place for me to go."

"That's terrible, Leon," said Raoulino. "I'm so sorry."

"It could have happened to your home, too," said Leon.

Raoulino looked at Basil and the cobra.

"Speaking for myself," the cobra said, "I will take that risk."

Basil and Raoulino nodded slowly.

"Yes," they said. "So will we."

Wally gave a huge sigh.

"I want to go home, too," he said sadly. "I have eight brothers and sisters back in Arizona, and I want to see them again. But I'm a desert animal. I don't think there are any ships that go to the desert."

"But there are hundred of cars and buses and trucks and trains," said Basil. "We'll find some way for you to travel. I'm sure we will."

Wally jumped up and gave Basil a huge grin.

"That's great," he said. "Just think of it. By the time the summer comes, we'll all be back home!"

"I can't wait to tell Sam about this!" said Basil.

All day long, the animals watched the window, but the little sparrow did not appear. The next two days it rained, but on the third day the sky cleared, and just as the sun came out, Sam landed on the windowsill.

The moment he saw her, Basil rushed to the window, chirping and twittering as fast as he could. When he stopped, Sam gave a low whistle and began chirping and twittering even faster. As soon as she finished, Basil turned to the others with a big smile and said, "She'll do it! She'll look for the ships, and she'll lead us to the harbor. And she'll find a hiding place for us, too."

"A hiding place?" said Raoulino. "What for?"

"We have to escape during breakfast," said Basil. "So it will be light outside. We don't want to be seen, so we'll have to hide somewhere during the day and travel to the harbor at night."

"Sam is right," Raoulino exclaimed. "I never thought of that!"

Raoulino was so excited he could hardly stand still. He hopped up and down, smiling at Sam and waving his tail. The sparrow bobbed her head at him, her black eyes shining. Then she moved closer to the window, looked carefully at the pictures of the flags, and flew away.

Weeks went by. Every day Sam came to the window and chirped to Basil.

"No ships yet," Basil always said.

Raoulino and Wally always stamped their feet and grumbled, but Basil only smiled and said, "Never mind. Maybe they'll be here tomorrow."

Raoulino thought of nothing but the escape. Often, instead of sleeping, he lay awake in the dark silence of the reptile house and went right on thinking. In the middle of one warm June night, he sat up, exclaiming, "We have to be sure to close the doors behind us when we jump out of our cages! If Stanley sees them hanging open, he'll know something is wrong."

The cobra stirred.

"That is a very good idea," he said, yawning. "Now close your eyes, and try to go to sleep. You will need all your energy when the time comes."

Raoulino settled down and closed his eyes. After a while, he began to dream. He dreamed he was standing at the top of a high hill. All around him were shiny, silvery green creatures that looked just like him. Their eight-sided scales gleamed in the moonlight, and when they turned to look at him, the pupils of their eyes flashed like black diamonds.

"Welcome home, Raoulino," they said, their voices roaring like a hurricane's winds. "Welcome home!"

Raoulino's heart overflowed with joy. He opened his mouth to answer, but his joy turned terror. Now the dream creatures were gray and furry, and their little eyes gleamed with an evil reddish light. They had changed into giant rats!

All of a sudden, the rats charged straight at him! Desperate with fear, Raoulino stood up on his hind legs and roared as loudly as he could. Flames shot out of his mouth, but the rats kept on coming. He roared again, even louder this time . . . and woke himself up!

Raoulino lay on his side, panting.

What a horrible dream, he thought. He looked around the reptile house. All the other animals were asleep. Moonlight streamed through the narrow windows. Raoulino sat up and sniffed the air.

"How strange," he said to himself. "I think I smell smoke."

Even though there were two big NO SMOKING signs on the walls, all the animals knew that Stanley sometimes sneaked a cigarette when he thought no other people could see him.

"But Stanley never comes here in the middle of the night," Raoulino said to himself.

He sniffed the air again. This time, he could hardly smell the smoke at all.

I must have imagined it, he thought, *because of the dream.*

Raoulino's mouth felt hot and dry, and he was very thirsty. He stood up, walked to his water dish, and took a big, refreshing drink. As he walked back to his sleeping spot, he noticed that the plants in his cage looked different. Their edges were curled and brown, as if they hadn't been given enough water, or as if they had been touched, very lightly, by a flame.

How very odd, he thought as he curled up on his soft, comfortable sand. *I wonder. . . .*

Suddenly, he gave an enormous yawn. Then another.

Before he could finish wondering, his eyes closed and he fell asleep.

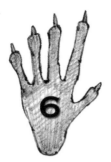

The next time Raoulino opened his eyes, the sun was shining brightly. As he sat up and stretched his tail, Sam swooped down onto the windowsill and began chirping at the top of her lungs. The noise woke Basil, who rushed to the front of his cage. As soon as she saw him, the little sparrow raised her left wing and pointed to the west.

Basil gave a loud whoop and started jumping up and down.

"Wake up, sir!" he yelled. "Wake up, Wally! The ships are in the harbor! The weather is good! Today's the day!"

Raoulino was so excited he couldn't speak. Basil was still jumping up and down, and Wally was punching the air and shouting, "Yes!"

"Basil! Wally! Calm down at once," commanded the cobra. "There is still much to do!"

He glided to the front of his cage and called "Trident!"

A bright-eyed young alligator, the biggest of them all, climbed out of the pool and hurried to the front of the alligator enclosure.

"Is today the day, sir?" he asked eagerly.

"Yes, Trident, it is," the cobra replied. "Are you ready?"

"You bet!" Trident replied. "They all know the plan. I stand on the highest rock and hold my tail up. That's the signal for quiet. When I drop my tail, they start to riot, and when I raise it again, they stop. At least I *hope* they stop," he added, sounding a bit worried. "Some of the guys, you know, sir, they can get a bit wild."

"You must do your best to make them understand the seriousness of the situation, Trident," said the cobra. "Our freedom depends upon it."

"Don't worry, sir," said Trident. "I'll do my best."

"That is all one can ask," the cobra said. "We will always be grateful."

"Good luck, sir," said Trident. "Good luck to all of you."

He gave the cobra a solemn nod and plunged back into the pool.

The cobra took a deep breath and looked at his friends.

"As you know, if Eileen brings our breakfasts, we will have to try to escape another day. But if Stanley brings them, we will be leaving very soon. Let us use the remaining time to compose ourselves. We must be calm and strong if the moment comes!"

He closed his eyes and began to sway back and forth, softly chanting something that sounded like "Om." Basil, too, put his head down, closed his eyes, and stood quietly. Wally kept on punching the air and muttering things like "Take that, you rats," under his breath.

Raoulino looked around the reptile house. He had been safe here for many months, and his heart thumped as he thought of the dangerous journey that lay ahead. He went to his special spot to rest. The calm feeling he always got from his stones started to flow through his body.

"My stones!" he thought, suddenly sitting up again. He dug them up carefully and placed them on the sand.

I can't take them with me, he thought, looking at them sadly. *We'll have to travel for days. I can't carry them in my mouth for that long, and I'll need all my feet for walking.*

He reached out and touched the stones gently. Once again, he felt strength, calm, and happiness flow into his heart.

"I'll be all right without them," he whispered, "but I can't just leave them here."

He thought for a moment. Then he smiled. Carefully, he pushed the stones to the corner of his cage. Using his tail, he drew a small heart around them. Right under them, in his very best printing, he wrote the words FOR EILEEN.

Then he hurried to the front of the cage and waited to see who would bring their breakfasts.

The reptile house was silent. All the other animals had moved to the front of their cages to watch the escape, even Leon, who was bright orange with excitement.

Raoulino's heart was hammering. Suddenly, he heard the clatter of the breakfast cart coming up the aisle.

"It's Stanley," said Basil, his voice shaking. "Get ready!"

"Ready, Trident!" said the cobra.

Trident climbed out of his pool and stood on a high flat rock from which he could see the entire reptile house. He raised his tail high. The other alligators, their eyes bright with excitement, lined up facing him.

The animals watched silently as Stanley, pushing the cart, made his way slowly up the aisle. He stopped at the frogs' cage, fed them, and locked their door. The next cage was Wally's!

There was a sharp click as the key turned in the lock, and Wally's door swung open. Stanley picked up Wally's empty water dish and put it on the cart. The moment his back was turned, Trident gave the signal.

Instantly, the reptile house was filled with wild splashes and earsplitting roars. Shouting furiously,

Stanley rushed away, leaving Wally's door wide open.

Quick as a flash, Wally jumped out, slamming the door behind him. He dashed down the corridor and disappeared.

"We did it!" Raoulino shouted. "Wally's free!"

There was an angry yell, and Stanley, red-faced, sweating, and lugging a big pail, hurried back into the room. He rushed to the alligators' pool and began throwing handfuls of food at them.

Trident raised his tail.

Immediately, the alligators quieted down and began eating. Stanley threw down the pail and stomped back to the cages.

"Stupid alligators," he muttered to himself. "I can't *wait* to get back to the bird house!"

Still muttering, he came up the aisle and stopped in front of Raoulino's cage. Raoulino's heart was pounding so hard he could hardly breathe as he watched Stanley unlock his door and reach for his water dish. He glanced across the room and saw Trident looking at him. The alligator nodded once and raised his tail. As soon as Stanley turned, Trident lowered his tail. The alligators began roaring and bellowing even louder than before.

Stanley dropped Raoulino's dish on the floor and raced out to get more food.

Raoulino crept to the edge of his cage and looked down. The floor seemed very far away. His legs were trembling.

"Jump, Raoulino," Basil shouted.

Raoulino jumped, flicking the door shut with his tail. For a few seconds he floated freely through the air. Then he crashed to the floor, scrambled to his feet, and started running down the corridor.

When he got to the end, his heart froze.

The iron door was shut!

"Raoulino! Over here!" said a voice.

Raoulino turned. For a moment he saw nothing. Then he saw Wally's face sticking out from under a bunch of pipes that lined the wall.

"Don't worry," whispered Wally as Raoulino crawled in and huddled beside him. "Soon they'll open the door for the visitors. There's always a little time before they start coming in, and we'll make a run for it then. Look! Stanley's at the cobra's cage now."

From his shadowy corner of the corridor, Raoulino saw Stanley reaching for the cobra's water dish. Raoulino could tell the cobra was pretending to be asleep. There were giggles and loud splashes from the alligator's pool.

"The alligators are getting restless," Raoulino said uneasily. "I'm not sure they're going to keep on listening to Trident."

"Neither am I," said Wally, sounding grim.

Trident started to give the signal. Before he could finish, another alligator, deep green and nearly as large as Trident, rose out of the water and climbed onto Trident's rock.

"Get off my rock, Igor," snarled Trident.

"Who's gonna make me?" Igor said with a sneer. "You're not tough enough to fight."

Trident growled. He stood up on his short, green legs and snapped his huge jaws.

Igor moved closer. Now Igor and Trident were nose to nose, snarling at each other. The other alligators were silent, watching them.

"Oh, no!" thought Raoulino. "They've forgotten all about us!"

Working quickly, Stanley took out the cobra's empty food dish and put in a full one. Raoulino's heart sank as he saw Stanley reach into his pocket for his key, so he could lock the cobra's door.

"The cobra's missed his chance," he said miserably. "Those dumb alligators have spoiled everything."

Suddenly, Igor sank his teeth deep into Trident's shoulder. Growls, roars, and shouts of "Let 'im have it, Igor," and "Get 'im, Trident," filled the reptile house. Stanley, his face purple with fury, rushed away, leaving the cobra's door wide open.

The great snake's golden eyes glittered when he saw the open door. Swiftly, he slid out of his cage to the floor. He reached up, slammed the door, and raced to the spot where Raoulino and Wally were hiding.

The three animals crouched in the shadows as Stanley came running down the corridor. He stopped for a moment, pulled out a handkerchief, and mopped his face. Something fell from his pocket and landed a few feet from Raoulino's nose, but Stanley didn't notice. He thrust the handkerchief back in his pocket and rushed out of the reptile house, leaving the iron door wide open behind him.

"He's gone for help," said the cobra. "And we must go, too, before he comes back."

"No," Raoulino whispered fiercely. "We can't leave Basil here!"

He looked around wildly. When he saw what had fallen from Stanley's pocket, he could hardly believe his eyes.

"Look!" he shouted, running to pick it up. "It's Stanley's key! Wally! You'll have to boost me up!"

Wally nodded and raced back to Basil's cage, the cobra right behind him. Bracing himself with his front legs, Wally got up on his back legs. Raoulino, holding the heavy key in his jaws, dashed down the aisle, scrambled up Wally's back, and climbed up to the lock.

"Go!" shouted Basil, his face pressed against the wire screen. "Stanley will be back any moment and you'll all be caught!"

Raoulino didn't answer. Gripping the wire mesh with all four of his claws, he bit down hard on the key and tried to push it into the opening in the lock. It didn't fit. Raoulino's stomach twisted.

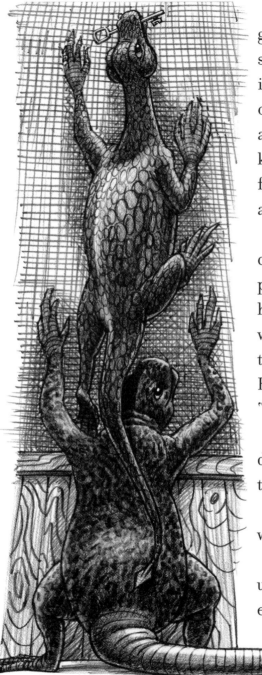

"The bumpy end goes in front!" shouted Basil. "Turn it around!" Raoulino opened his mouth and tried to turn the key with his right front leg; it slipped and fell to the floor.

Instantly, the cobra glided over, picked up the key in his mouth the right way, and gave it back to Raoulino. "Steady, Raoulino," he said. "You can do it!"

Raoulino took a deep breath and tried again.

Still, the key would not go in.

"It must be upside down," shouted Basil, his small,

striped body quivering. "Turn it the other way!"

The alligators were making so much noise the whole reptile house seemed to be shaking.

"Hurry, Raoulino. Hurry!" called Wally. "Stanley will be back any second."

Raoulino's legs were trembling. *I've got to get it right this time*, he thought. *I've just got to!*

As carefully as he could, he turned the key around. Then he clamped it tightly between his teeth and slipped it into the lock.

This time, it fit!

"Turn it this way," Basil yelled, turning his head to the right.

Raoulino twisted his head.

The lock clicked, and the door swung open.

"Come on, Basil!" panted Raoulino. "You're free!"

Basil jumped from his cage, and the four of them raced down the corridor. When they were nearly at the entrance, Sam flew in through the door, chirping madly.

"Hide," screamed Basil. "Stanley's coming back!"

Raoulino and his friends dived behind the pipes just as Stanley and three or four other keepers, all of them carrying big nets, dashed through the doorway and thundered down the corridor.

Sam circled low, chirping again.

"There are bushes along the outside wall of the reptile house," Basil translated. "Hide behind them as soon as you go out the door. When it's safe, Sam will lead us to the hiding place."

Raoulino and his friends crouched together under the pipes. Splashes and frenzied roars were still coming from the alligator pool.

Minutes passed.

Suddenly, they heard a cascade of clear chirps.

Raoulino, Basil, Wally, and the cobra crept out of the reptile house and dashed into the space between the bushes and the brick wall.

Sam chirped again. Moving as carefully as they could, the four friends followed Sam across the park, doing their best to hide behind tree trunks, bushes, and benches as they went. Suddenly, just as they were about to leave the shelter of a big oak tree, they heard footsteps pounding along a nearby path.

"It's Stanley!" whispered Raoulino. "He's coming after us!"

Basil turned quickly. But it wasn't Stanley. Two young men in shorts and black sneakers were running up the path.

"Runners," said Basil briefly, "I've read about them. They're not looking for us."

When the runners had gone, the four animals, with Sam leading the way, moved cautiously through a field of tall grass. The sunshine was warm on their backs, and when Raoulino looked up, he saw fluffy little clouds floating in the bright blue sky.

"Oh, isn't it lovely!" he murmured.

"Do not speak now," commanded the cobra. "Move as quickly as you can!"

Soon the field was behind them. They were under some trees where it was dark and cool, and their steps made no sound as they crossed a dense carpet of pine needles. As they passed the last tree, Sam began chirping furiously. Basil listened, and his face turned very pale.

"What's wrong?" Raoulino asked.

"Sam says that Stanley and another man are coming this way!"

"We've got to get to the hiding place!" Raoulino said with a cry. Running as quickly as they could, they all followed Sam up a little hill. The sparrow flew behind a bush and showed them an opening in the rock so small that they could only crawl in two at a time. When they did, they found themselves in a dark, damp, chilly cave.

"What an awful place," said Wally, sneezing violently. "I hope we don't have to stay here very long."

As quickly as they could, tripping and stumbling in the darkness, the four friends made their way to the back of the cave. Here and there a narrow ray of sunlight shone through a hole in the ceiling, but the cave was dim and full of shadows. The floor was scattered with sharp rocks. Raoulino and his friends hurried to the back of the cave and crouched, panting, behind the biggest rocks they could find.

For a few moments, everything was silent. Then

Raoulino heard squeaks and an odd rustling sound coming from overhead. He looked up and saw a small, upside down face.

Then another.

And another.

The roof of the cave was covered with bats!

Raoulino's stomach flipped.

These bats were a lot bigger than the friendly little bats on his island.

And they looked mean.

The rustling and squeaking grew more frenzied. A few of the bigger bats swooped down to get a better look at Raoulino and his friends, but they didn't come too close.

"Bow!" whispered the cobra.

"What?" Raoulino whispered back.

"Bow to them," the cobra said again, touching his own head to the ground. "We must show them that we don't mean any harm."

Raoulino, Basil, and Wally bent their heads.

"Good," whispered the cobra. "Now stay this way until I tell you to rise."

The four animals stood with their heads bent. Gradually, the rustling and squeaking quieted down.

"Rise," whispered the cobra.

Raoulino and his friends looked up. Three big bats were sitting on a high ledge, peering down at them. The cobra nodded politely to the bats. They squeaked nervously, and then slowly nodded in return.

"We are safe now, I think," the cobra said softly. "Most bats are shy creatures, though they often look quite frightening. We must be careful not to make any sudden movements and scare them again, for their noise may alert the keepers that we are here."

Raoulino, Basil, and Wally nodded politely to the bats. They could hear the crunch of footsteps and the faint murmur of voices coming from outside as people continued to search for them. Suddenly, the bushes were pushed aside, and the bright beam of a big flashlight pierced the darkness.

Raoulino caught his breath and scrunched down behind his rock, making himself as small as possible. Disturbed and angry, the squeaking bats zoomed in every direction. Raoulino shuddered and pressed himself closer to the floor.

The beam of light traveled slowly throughout the cave.

"It's just a bunch of bats," yelled Stanley.

"Maybe the animals we're looking for are hiding behind those rocks at the back," a second voice said.

"Are you kidding?" snapped Stanley. "If they were in here, those bats would be going crazy. They were fine till I shone the light on them."

"Yeah. You're right. Let's look near the lake."

The flashlight clicked off, leaving the animals once again in darkness, and the footsteps crunched away. The bats stopped zooming and squeaking and reattached themselves to the ceiling.

"Oh, sir," said Wally, "you saved us! You are so wise!"

"Yes," said the cobra. "That worked out well. But we must rest now. We have a long night ahead of us, and I fear that the most dangerous part of our escape is yet to come."

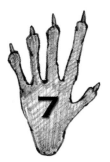

Much later, when the moon had risen and the night wind rustled through the trees, Sam flew into the cave and landed beside Basil, chirping and hopping up and down in excitement.

"Sam says the searchers have moved to the other side of the park, and there's nobody else around," said Basil. "It's safe for us to leave!"

The four friends hurried out of the cave and started down the hill. The moon shone faintly, and here and there a streetlight glimmered, but the park was very dark. The cobra delicately sniffed the night air.

"I smell rain," he said softly. "I'm afraid there will be a storm before morning."

Raoulino and his friends made their way through the darkened park. Around them they could hear the sounds of night-hunting animals. A family of raccoons, foraging for food under a picnic table, stared at them curiously as passed.

They crawled steadily on. When they had left the pine forest far behind them and crossed a wide, grassy meadow, Raoulino began to hear a low, rumbling roar that started softly, grew louder, and then softer again.

"Basil, what's that noise?" he whispered.

Basil and Sam chirped briefly. Then Basil said, "It's the traffic. Sam says we're almost at the edge of the park. Look!"

Raoulino, the cobra, and Wally peered through the darkness. In the light from a street lamp, they could see where the grass stopped growing and a sidewalk began. Beyond the sidewalk, they saw a smooth, black street. As Raoulino and his friends crossed the last bit of grass and stepped onto the sidewalk, the rumbling sound began again, and dozens of white headlights lit up the street. Cars, trucks, and buses whizzed by.

"Wow!" said Raoulino. "They move so fast!"

"Everything moves fast in a city," said Basil. He paused for a moment, took a deep breath, and said, "Sam says we have to cross that street."

"Cross the street!" said Raoulino with a gasp. "How can we do that?"

"Those cars will kill us!" Wally cried.

"Sam has a plan," said Basil. "Do you see that red light?"

Raoulino, Wally, and the cobra looked in the direction Basil pointed and saw a round red light shining on the opposite side of the street.

"Now watch what happens," Basil said. All the animals kept their eyes on the red light. Two cars zoomed by, and Raoulino and his friends felt the breeze from the moving traffic on their faces. As they watched, the red light disappeared, a green light flashed on, and the traffic slowed to a stop.

"You see," whispered Basil, "when the light turns green for us the traffic stops. That's our chance to cross the street."

Raoulino sighed with relief.

"Then it's much easier than I thought," he said.

"Not really," said Basil. "Watch again."

They all looked back at the light. In a few moments, it turned red again, and the traffic sped past them.

"It doesn't stay green very long, does it?" Wally whispered.

"No, it doesn't," Basil said. "But it's our only chance."

The four animals crept closer to the curb.

"There's one more thing," whispered Basil. "When we cross the street, we've got to go underneath the cars and trucks."

"Underneath? Why?" Wally asked.

"Because the people might see us in the light from their headlights," said Basil.

"Why can't we go behind them?" Raoulino asked.

"Another car might come along and shine its lights on us," Basil explained. "Now get ready. And when I say 'Go,' run for your lives!"

Raoulino forced himself to the edge of the curb. Basil, the cobra, and Wally lined up beside him, while Sam fluttered anxiously overhead. All at once, Raoulino felt a sharp pain as a jagged rock struck his back and bounced off the curb.

"Got him!" somebody yelled.

A gang of boys was running up the street, laughing and shouting and throwing whatever they could find at Raoulino and his friends. A tall thin boy with shiny yellow hair threw another rock at Raoulino, and a darker, shorter boy hurled an empty beer can at Wally. The can smacked into Wally's tail and clattered away.

A bonfire of rage exploded in Raoulino's chest. He spun around, but just as he started for the boys, the light turned green, a big bus stopped at the curb, and Basil shouted, "Go!"

The four friends plunged off the curb and dove under the bus. The gasoline fumes smelled awful and made Raoulino feel sick, but he kept going, running faster than he ever had before. He dashed out from beneath the bus and darted under a little sports car, gasping as he felt the heat radiating from the powerful engine just above his head. He shot out from under the sports car and ran underneath an enormous truck. Suddenly, Raoulino's right front foot hit a patch of something wet and shiny; he skidded and fell, bruising his side.

The light's going to turn green for the traffic any minute, he thought, terrified.

He leaped to his feet. Horns blared; the gigantic wheels began to turn. With lungs bursting, Raoulino raced out from under the truck and ran for the sidewalk. He heard two soft thuds as Wally and the cobra landed beside him. They were safe!

For a few moments, Raoulino stayed flat on the hard pavement, his heart thudding, his chest heaving as he tried to catch his breath. Then he sat up and looked around for Basil.

"Basil?" he said softly. "Basil?"

There was no answer.

Basil wasn't there.

Raoulino, Wally, and the cobra were huddled beneath a mailbox waiting for Basil. For what seemed like hours, they had been staring at the street, watching the lights change from green to red to green again, hoping each time that Basil would come leaping over the curb.

But Basil had not come.

"He's so small," Wally said, shaking his head. "If a car or a truck hit him. . . ."

Raoulino's stomach clenched as he thought of his friend lying hurt and alone somewhere in the city.

"We've waited long enough," he said firmly, getting to his feet. "We've got to go back and look for him."

"You are right, Raoulino," said the cobra. "We

have crossed that street once. We can do it again."

Wally gulped.

"S . . . sure we can," he said, trying his best to sound cheerful. "It . . . it'll probably be easier the second time."

Raoulino, Wally, and the cobra crept out from beneath the mailbox and stood at the edge of the curb, hearts racing and muscles tensed.

Cars, buses, and trucks streamed past.

"We can do it," Wally kept muttering under his breath. "We can do it."

The light flashed green; the traffic began to slow.

"Get ready," said the cobra.

All of a sudden, they heard an explosion of joyful chirping, and Sam zoomed out of the sky and landed beside them.

"Sam!" cried Raoulino. "Have you seen Basil?"

The sparrow nodded quickly and pointed at the street with her wing. Raoulino peered hopefully into the street. After a few moments he saw a shadow moving toward them under the cars. The shadow came closer.

It was Basil!

Pale but smiling, Basil leaped onto the curb. Raoulino, the cobra, and Wally crowded around him, hugging him and pounding him on the back.

Suddenly, Wally stepped back with a horrified look and stammered, "Basil . . . the tip of your tail . . . it. . . .it's gone!"

"Of course, it is," said Basil. "Those boys chased me for blocks until the one with the yellow hair finally caught me and grabbed me by my tail. He wouldn't let go, so I disconnected a bit of it."

His face lit with a mischievous grin.

"You should have heard him squawk when it came off in his hand and started wiggling! The boys all got scared and ran away, but I didn't have any idea where I was. It's a good thing Sam found me and showed me how to get back here."

"But your tail. . . ." wailed Wally.

"Don't worry," said Basil. "It will grow back. My Uncle Theophilus disconnected his *whole* tail twice before he was twenty, and he has a fine tail. Now let's go. We've wasted enough time already."

The animals hurried down the street. When they had gone about a dozen blocks, they heard the click of high-heeled shoes coming up behind them.

"Quick! Hide in the shadows and do not move," the cobra said with a hiss.

The four of them melted into the black shadows between two buildings and stood still. Two women, laughing and talking together, walked right by them and kept on going.

"Look at that," whispered Raoulino when the two women were almost out of sight. "They walked right by, and they didn't even see us!"

"Sam told me people in cities are like that," Basil whispered back. "They move fast, but they don't notice much."

The animals kept walking. They came to another street, but this was a narrow one, with no traffic, and they crossed it easily. On and on they went. The air was beginning to smell bad, and the breeze blew pieces of trash and old newspapers down the street.

"Where are the people?" asked Raoulino, when they had crossed two more empty streets. "There's nobody around here!"

Basil chirped a question to Sam, who answered with a few quick peeps.

"Sam says people don't come to this part of the city at night," Basil said.

The wind blew a torn sheet of newspaper into Raoulino's face.

"I can see why," he said, pushing the paper away.

They kept walking.

As they approached another corner, they heard a low, grumbling roar. A big white bus appeared in front of them, turned right, and drove down the street.

"Look at that!" exclaimed Wally. "That big car came out of that building over there!"

"It's not a car," said Basil. "It's a bus. Come on! I have an idea!"

Moving quickly, Basil led them to the large

building that the bus had come from. It was very easy to look inside, since the whole front wall was missing. They saw a large room with a dozen big white buses lined up against the back wall, each with a different sign over the front window. Raoulino was carefully spelling out the words.

"Albany, New York," he read. "Boston, Massachusetts. Detroit, Michigan. Basil, what does it mean?"

Basil's eyes were sparkling.

"It means," he said, "that we've found a way for Wally to travel. Look at the next to the last bus."

Raoulino looked. "Phoenix, Arizona," he read out loud.

"Arizona?" said Wally. "That . . . that big bus is going to Arizona?"

"Yes!" said Basil joyfully.

"This is indeed a stroke of great good fortune," said the cobra. "We must make the most of it."

The friends peered around the room. A big, red box with the word SODA written on it stood just inside the entrance. Sam landed quietly on top of it, while Raoulino, Basil, Wally, and the cobra darted into the dark space between the box and the wall.

"Careful," whispered the cobra. "There are lots of people over there."

Raoulino and his friends peeked out and saw several rows of benches lined up right next to the box. The benches were crowded with people, most of them holding bags or boxes on their laps. Suitcases, backpacks, and duffel bags lay on the floor beside their feet.

"How am I ever going to get past them?" whispered Wally. "If I run to the bus, someone will surely see me."

The four friends looked at each other in dismay.

"I think those things on the ground belong to the people," Basil said slowly. "So they'll probably pick them up and carry them onto the bus. Maybe you could get inside one of the big bags and travel that way."

"But there are so many bags," said Wally. "How can I tell which one is going to Arizona?"

"NOW BOARDING FOR BOSTON," a loud voice called.

All of a sudden a huge pair of hands reached down, snatching up the large bag in front of Basil and Raoulino. The two friends scooted farther along the wall and came to a pink duffel bag.

"It's my birthday, and I want my presents," wailed the little girl sitting on a bench above the bag.

"I told you, Stacey," said a woman with a tired voice, "you'll get your presents when we get to Phoenix. You're having your party at Grandma's this year."

Basil nudged Raoulino.

"That's it!" whispered Raoulino.

Clinging close to the wall, Raoulino and Basil hurried back to their friends.

"That one," whispered Basil, pointing to the pink bag. "It's going to Arizona!"

"Hurry, Wally," hissed the cobra. "You must leave at once!"

"N . . . now?" said Wally. "But I don't even have time to say good-bye!"

"You don't have to," said Raoulino. "We're your friends. We understand. Now go!"

For an instant, Wally stood frozen.

"Good-bye," he whispered, his eyes filling with tears. "I'll never forget you."

Then he turned and ran as quickly and stealthily as he could toward the pink bag. "I want my presents NOW!" screamed Stacey, jumping off the bench and stamping her pink and purple sneakers.

"NOW BOARDING FOR PHOENIX," said the loud voice.

Wally was moving faster than he ever had before. He reached the pink duffel bag, pulled the strings apart with his sharp claws, and darted inside.

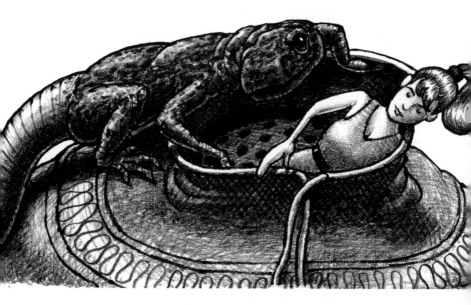

"NOW! NOW! NOW!" shouted Stacey, kicking at the bench.

"STOP THAT! THE BUS IS LEAVING!" yelled Stacey's mother, snatching up the bag, closing it, and retying the strings. "I SAID STOP KICKING THAT BENCH!"

She grabbed Stacey by the hand, marched her off to the bus, and gave the pink bag to the driver, who stowed it in the luggage compartment and slammed the compartment door shut.

Stacey, her mother, and all the other passengers got onto the bus. The driver took his seat, the door closed, and with a roar and a flash of headlights, the big bus rolled out of the building.

Sam, Basil, Raoulino, and the cobra slipped out of the bus station.

"Isn't it wonderful?" said Basil. "Wally's on his way home!"

"Yes, it is," said Raoulino.

"It is truly a wondrous event," said the cobra, "but we cannot stop to celebrate. We must get to the harbor before sunrise."

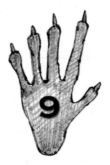

The air began to grow cooler. After a while, a sharp breeze sprang up and Raoulino smelled the salty tang of the sea.

We must be near the harbor, he thought happily.

He heard a faint chattering sound coming from farther up the street.

"Is that Sam?" asked Raoulino. "What is she saying?"

"That wasn't Sam," said Basil, sounding worried. "I don't know what it was!"

The three animals moved cautiously down the street. All of a sudden Raoulino saw a furry creature with a long pink tail dash through the pool of light beneath a streetlight.

It was a rat.

The biggest one he'd ever seen.

"Did you see that?" said Basil, panting.

"Yes," said the cobra. "But perhaps the rat did not see us. We must keep alert and move as fast as we can."

Basil and the cobra started moving faster, glancing around anxiously as they went. Raoulino tried to keep up with them, but it was getting harder and harder for him to move. His body felt so heavy, it was hard for him to take even one step, and his chest and his throat burned with every breath. There was an odd smell of smoke in the air.

That's strange, he thought. *I don't see anything burning. Maybe I'll feel better if I have some food.* He sniffed at the few skinny green weeds that poked up through the cracks in the hard, gray street, but they were covered with dirt and smelled awful.

All of a sudden, Raoulino heard the chattering sound again.

Heart hammering, he raced to catch up with his friends. His chest felt as if it were on fire. He zoomed around the corner and saw the cobra, his head raised and his hood spread wide. He was curled in a protective circle around Basil, who was rigid with fear. A dozen big brown rats surrounded them, their evil little eyes glowing red in the light from the streetlight, their sharp teeth gleaming.

Raoulino's mind was whirling. Frantically, he searched the darkness. A metal can filled with garbage was standing at the edge of the sidewalk.

If I knock that can over, the noise might frighten the rats away, he thought. *Or, the rats might start eating the garbage and forget all about Basil and the cobra. Basil once told me they like garbage.*

Bracing himself with his tail, Raoulino stood up and pressed his front legs and the top of his head against the can and shoved with all his strength.

The can didn't budge.

He set his jaw and pushed again. Suddenly, the heat in his chest seemed to flood through his whole body. Raoulino pushed harder. The can slid off the sidewalk, crashed to the ground, and rolled down the street, clattering and banging as it went.

The rats squealed and started running.

Raoulino dashed to the tree, dug his claws into its bark, and began to climb.

In a flash, the cobra pushed Basil to the foot of the tree.

"Climb!" the cobra shouted, his hissing voice almost lost in the sound of the rising wind. "Climb, Basil!" The cobra sped down the street after the rats, his hood spread, venom spouting from his fangs.

Raoulino scrambled his way onto a stout branch near the top of the tree.

"This is a good, strong branch," he called back to Basil. "There's room here for you, too."

There was no answer. Raoulino crawled to the edge of the branch and looked down. Basil had fallen! He was lying on the ground, surrounded by six vicious-looking rats.

As Raoulino watched, his mouth dry with fear, Basil dragged himself shakily to his feet. He took a deep breath and began to run in circles. All of a sudden, he detached the rest of his tail, which began to wriggle all by itself!

The rats took a few steps back, staring at the tail and chattering uneasily among themselves.

"Good boy!" breathed Raoulino, clinging to the branch as it tossed back and forth in the wind.

A few minutes passed.

The tail started to slow down.

Raoulino was gripping the tree trunk so hard, his legs were aching.

"Why doesn't he do something else?" Raoulino said to himself. Then his heart grew cold.

"Because he can't," he realized. "He's not a fighter. As soon as the rats see this is all that he can do, they'll attack. But how I can stop them?"

The wind blew harder, tossing Raoulino's branch up and down. Raoulino was tingling from the end of his nose to the tip of his tail. His chest felt as if it were filling with flames. Then, with a sound like *whump*, both sides of his body suddenly opened and spread out like two fans.

"Wings!" he said gasping, scarcely able to believe what was happening. "I have wings!" He was so totally, utterly, flabbergasted that he forgot to hold onto the branch. The wind filled his wings as if they were sails, pulled him out of the tree, and tossed him head over tail into the sky.

Raoulino's heart pounded with fright as the wind blew him through the air. He lifted his left wing and moved to the right. He raised his right wing and moved to the left.

I'm flying, he thought in amazement. *I'm really flying!*

He looked down. In the light from one of the street lamps he saw Basil, the rats still surrounding him. Pumping his new found wings as hard as he could, Raoulino sped down toward his friend.

"Basil," he started to shout, "I'm h. . . ."

Before he could finish, a great sheet of flame shot out of his mouth, lit up the sky for a moment, and turned into a thick cloud of bright red smoke.

Coughing and choking, nearly blinded by the smoke, Raoulino zigzagged wildly through the air.

"What's happening to me?" he cried, frantically beating his wings. "What's going on?"

The smoke cleared quickly. Raoulino saw Basil staring up at him, his mouth wide open. Beside him,

Sam was hopping up and down, chirping madly.

The rats were gone.

"Raoulino!" Basil called. "Is . . . is that really you?"

"Yes, it's me!" Raoulino called back. "Look out, I'm coming down!"

Lowering his head, he started flying down to his friends, but as he neared the treetop he suddenly turned ice-cold with terror. He was coming down much too fast! He didn't know how to stop! He was going to smash face-first into the street!

As he sped past the branches, he heard Sam chirping at the top of her lungs. Basil was yelling something, too, but the wind was so loud in his ears, Raoulino could hardly hear him.

"Raise your head, curve your wings, and drop your tail!" Basil roared again. "Sam says to raise your head, curve your wings, and drop your tail."

Instantly, Raoulino lifted his head, pointed his tail at the ground, and curved his wings. Immediately, he felt the wind push against his body, and he began to slow down. For a moment it seemed that he was just hanging in the air. Then his tail hit the street, his back legs thumped, his front legs bumped—he had landed!

Basil and Sam came running up to him, their eyes enormous.

"Raoulino!" Basil gasped. "You . . . you're a dragon!"

"Yes," Raoulino said panting, blowing out a little puff of orange smoke with each breath. "I must be. But I can't believe it! Everyone said they're extinct!"

He looked anxiously at Basil.

"Do you think I'm the only one?"

Basil was silent for a moment.

"I don't think so," he said finally. "You must have had a dragon mother, who laid your egg. If there was one dragon, there must be others."

"And I know where to find them!" Raoulino broke in excitedly. "Remember when I told you that my great-grandmother said she had seen one at the top of the mountain when she was young? No one believed her, but I bet she really did. Maybe my egg just rolled down the mountain, and that's why my mother found it!"

Raoulino's heart was flooded with joy. *When I get home*, he thought, *I'll see my dear lizard family, and I'll find my dragon family, too. Nothing can stop me now!*

"Raoulino!" said a voice. "Is that you?"

Raoulino turned and saw the cobra gliding up the street. The snake's eyes were like two huge, glowing lamps.

"Yes, sir, it's me!" Raoulino called happily. "I'm a dragon! I can breathe fire, and I can fly, too! Did you see me?"

"I did," the cobra replied. "This world is truly full of wonders. But if you are a dragon, there are things I must tell you. Things that every dragon must know. . . ."

Suddenly, Raoulino heard footsteps coming from

the next block. There was a shout, then a crash, and the tinkle of broken glass. The shouts and footsteps grew louder, and a gang of boys carrying sticks turned the corner and came up the street.

"Hide," the cobra said. "Quickly!"

Sam flew up and landed silently on a windowsill. The others slid into the shadows and pressed themselves against the ground. The shouts and footsteps grew louder as the boys came closer.

Raoulino's heart was beating quickly. There were at least eight big boys in the gang, and as they walked under the streetlight, Raoulino recognized the boy who had thrown the can at Wally. Right behind him was the yellow-haired boy who had broken off a piece of Basil's tail.

Raoulino shook with anger. Flames were leaping in his chest!

"I'll fix them!" he muttered to himself. "They're going to be very sorry they did that!"

Slowly, he started edging away from his friends.

"Raoulino, don't go after them!" said the cobra. "There's no time! We've got to get to our ships!"

But Raoulino didn't listen. He could think of nothing but the white-hot anger burning in his chest.

"I'm a dragon," he said to himself, "and dragons don't hide. They fight!"

Careful to stay in the shadows, Raoulino took off, and began circling just over the boys' heads. Below him, the boys were pushing one another and shouting. As Raoulino watched, one of them snatched a bottle out of a trash can and smashed it in the street.

And they think reptiles are bad! Raoulino thought furiously. *They're the ones who should be locked up in cages!*

He swooped down from the clouds and shot a giant sheet of orange flame a tail-length above the boys' heads. Shrieking and screaming, they dropped their sticks and fled down the street. Raoulino, flying right behind them, burst into laughter as the yellow-haired boy tripped and fell flat on his face.

"Wait for me!" the boy shouted. But his friends kept on running and didn't even look back. As the boy stumbled to his feet, Raoulino swooped down and began whizzing around his head. A strange, fierce, powerful happiness swept over him as he saw the boy's face turn white with terror.

He turned a wild cartwheel in the air and started flying back to his friends. As he zoomed along, he looked down and saw a thin, hungry-looking cat hurrying along the empty street. Raoulino's flames sizzled in his chest. Roaring, he plunged down through the sky and sent a spray of bright red fire over the cat's head. The animal yowled with fright and raced off.

Raoulino laughed loudly as he watched the cat run away, its ragged fur standing on end, its scrawny tail tucked between its legs.

Suddenly, Raoulino felt a sharp, stabbing pain in his heart. He blinked; for a moment he felt as if he had just awakened from a dream.

Why did I do that? he wondered. *That poor cat wasn't bothering me. What's. . . .*

Before he could finish his thought, he heard a sharp bark. He turned and saw a big, furry gray dog, with a long pointed nose, come around the corner. Raoulino's flames burned hotter. Without warning, he dove down, roaring and breathing fire. The dog gave a terrified yelp, and ran away, limping because one of his back legs was lame.

Raoulino laughed so hard, he nearly fell out of the sky. All of a sudden, he felt the stabbing pain in his heart again.

"What's happening?" he asked himself. "Why did I frighten that poor dog?"

"I did it because I'm a dragon," Raoulino said to himself. "And that's what dragons DO!"

He soared higher and headed back toward his friends. As he skimmed along, he noticed that wire trash baskets filled with garbage were standing on every corner. Their round openings looked like the hoops the children from his island used to play their ball game. Laughing, Raoulino flew down a little lower, took aim at a basket, and breathed out a jet of fire.

"Two points!" Raoulino shouted as the flame shot into the center of the basket. He zoomed over the city streets, shooting at every basket he passed.

Suddenly, the quiet night was split by the loudest sound Raoulino had ever heard—a horrible screaming roar that rattled his teeth and shook every bone in his body. He turned around quickly and looked back. All the trash baskets were blazing like torches! As Raoulino watched, the horrible sound grew even louder, and an enormous red truck raced around the corner and came to a halt beside one of the burning trash baskets. The truck gave a final *whoop*, and the terrible sound stopped.

People in black coats and hats began jumping off the sides of the truck. They pulled a long hose from the truck, attached it to a silver-colored stump that stood at the edge of the street, and aimed the hose at the burning can. A gush of water burst from the hose, and the fire went out, forming a big cloud of smoke that rose into the sky. A huge puddle of water flooded the street. The people leaped back onto the truck, and it sped to the flaming basket on the next corner and stopped again.

Coughing, his eyes tearing from the nasty, garbage-smelling smoke, Raoulino flew along the street, looking for his friends.

As he got to the middle of the block, a voice called, "Raoulino?"

He landed quickly and looked around, but he saw no one. A moment later, Basil and the cobra slipped out from beneath a parked car and hurried over to him.

"Raoulino!" cried Basil. "We're so glad to see you! You were gone for so long! We didn't know what had happened to you!"

The wind gusted and blew the thick black smoke in their faces. They all started to cough. Raoulino saw that both his friends were dripping wet and shivering with cold.

This is all my fault, he thought sadly, and the sharp pain stabbed his heart again.

"Did you see what happened?" asked Basil as they hurried to the next street. "All the trash baskets started burning. The cobra and I hid under a car, and when the people put the fire out, they flooded the street. We nearly drowned!"

Raoulino glanced at the cobra, who was looking at him with sad golden eyes. It seemed to Raoulino that the great snake somehow knew that he was the one who had set the fires.

"He *can't* know," Raoulino said to himself. "He wasn't even *there!*"

He turned back to Basil.

"Yes . . . um . . . I saw it," he said. "I mean, I saw the fires and the truck, but I didn't see you."

Raoulino took a quick look around the empty street.

"Where's Sam?" he asked.

"We're not sure," said Basil. "Just before the fires started, she flew down to the harbor. It's almost morning, and she wanted to make sure that our ships were still there."

"She should have come back by now," said the cobra. "We will have to wait for her."

The three friends crept back into the shadows and stared up at the empty sky.

They waited for a long time. The moon had set and the stars were dimming in the sky when they heard a soft, unhappy cheep, and Sam landed on the sidewalk. Raoulino, Basil, and the cobra rushed over to greet her, but the little sparrow just stared silently at the ground, her wings drooping.

Basil said something to her in bird language, but she didn't answer. Basil chirped again, louder this time. Sam sighed and looked up, chirping so softly that Raoulino could hardly hear her.

Basil gasped, turning so pale that his small dark face looked almost yellow.

"Basil," said the cobra, very calmly, "what did Sam tell you?"

Basil swallowed hard.

"She said that she flew down to the harbor to make sure that none of our ships had sailed," he answered in a trembling voice. "Your ship is still there, sir, and so is Raoulino's. But . . . but my ship is gone."

The pain stabbed Raoulino's heart so sharply, he thought it would split in two.

"Oh, Basil," he burst out, "I'm so sorry! This is all my fault. I went off to chase those boys, and you had to wait for me. And then you had to wait until the people put out the fires and . . . and . . . I was the one who started them. I was just playing . . . I didn't think. . . ."

"It is my fault as well," the cobra said, looking sadder than Raoulino had ever seen him. "I should have made you listen. I was going to warn you."

"Warn me, sir? About what?" Raoulino asked.

"Dragonosterone," the cobra replied.

"Dragonosterone?" Raoulino repeated. "What's that?"

"It flows in the blood of all dragons," the cobra said with a sigh. "It's what gives them their powers." He sighed again. "But it also makes them love to fight. They begin to enjoy bullying other creatures. Then they start attacking them for no reason at all."

Raoulino remembered how badly he had wanted to fight the gang of boys. He thought of the strange, wild happiness he'd felt when he'd scared the cat and the dog.

"Yes," he whispered. "That's what happened to me."

The cobra nodded.

"Many dragons, the wiser ones, soon see this is wrong. They teach themselves not to do it. But many others do not, and *those* dragons have caused so much trouble over the years that *all* dragons, the good *and* the bad, have been hunted down everywhere. So many were killed that we all believed they were extinct."

The great snake took another breath. His eyes had lost their brightness and looked like chips of dull yellow stone. "I should have warned you," he said. "Then you would have been ready to fight against those bad feelings when they came."

"It wasn't your fault," said Raoulino. "I was the one who bullied the other animals and set the fires. I should have known better."

He sighed and looked down at his claws. *What a terrible dragon I turned out be*, he thought. *I've caused a whole lot of trouble, and I made Basil miss his ship.*

For a moment he felt even worse than he had the day he was captured and brought to the zoo.

"But I didn't do *everything* wrong," he said to himself. "I *did* save Basil from the rats. And I'm going to save him this time, too!"

The stabbing pain disappeared. Power surged from the tip of Raoulino's nose to the end of his tail, and out to the very edge of his wings, making him feel stronger than ever.

"Basil," he said excitedly. "Ask Sam if she knows where your ship is now!"

"Why should I do that?" Basil asked, sounding very tired.

"Because I'm going to fly you there on my back!" said Raoulino.

Basil's pale face turned a bright, healthy brown. Quickly, he turned and said something in bird language to Sam, who answered with a stream of joyful cheeps.

"Sam says the boat is heading north! She's going to fly with us!" Basil cried.

The cobra looked up at the sky. A thin line of light showed that daylight was coming, but the sky was still dark and full of heavy clouds. The air was thick and very still.

"It's going to storm, Raoulino," the cobra said. "It might be very dangerous to fly now, especially with Basil on your back. Are you sure you can do this?"

Raoulino smiled at him. "I'm sure, sir. I am a dragon, after all. And I'm a much wiser dragon than I was a little while ago."

The cobra looked at him carefully for a moment, without saying a word. His golden eyes began to glow.

"Yes," he said, "I can see that from now on, you will always try to do what is right."

"Yes, sir," said Raoulino. "I only have to listen to my heart."

The cobra smiled at him and Raoulino smiled back.

"And now," said the cobra, "I must get to my ship."

Raoulino stared at the cobra. A lump formed in his throat as he realized the time had come to say good-bye. Before he could speak, Basil cried out, "Oh, sir, I can't believe it. We will never see each other again!"

"You cannot be sure of that, Basil," said the cobra kindly. "Remember, our homes were thousands of miles apart, but still we met and became good friends. If it is meant for us to meet again, we will! Now you two must go, and I, too, must travel home. Basil, will you please ask Sam to tell me how to get to my ship?"

Basil turned to Sam, and the two of them chirped back and forth.

"Sam says your ship is docked one block from here, sir. It's the ninth ship in the row, and it's called the SS *Bengali*. It's a big white ship, and it has a flag with orange, white, and green stripes with a blue circle painted on the bow."

The great snake's golden eyes gleamed.

"Ah, yes. The people in the village near my jungle carried a flag like that on festival days. It will be so good to see it again! Basil, please give my thanks to Sam."

Basil chirped to Sam, while the cobra gave the little bird a deep bow. Then the snake raised his hooded head, and touched it gently to Basil's and Raoulino's foreheads.

"Go, my dear friends," he said. "Go before the storm begins!"

He bowed once to each of them, then turned his

face away and began gliding toward his ship.

For a moment, Basil, Raoulino, and Sam stood silently, watching him. Then the sparrow chirped loudly again. A slight wind stirred the thick, heavy air.

The cobra is right, thought Raoulino. *A storm is coming.*

"Hurry," he said to Basil. "Climb onto my back. We don't have much time!"

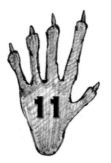

Raoulino lowered his tail to the ground. He could feel Basil's claws tickling as he stepped lightly onto Raoulino's tail and walked up to his back. Lying down as flat as he could, Basil tightened his front legs around Raoulino's neck, and pressed his back legs into Raoulino's sides.

"Is this all right?" he asked.

"Perfect," said Raoulino.

Thunder rumbled in the distance, and the breeze was picking up. Raoulino could feel Basil's frightened heart thudding against his back.

"Don't worry," Raoulino said cheerfully. "I'll get you to your ship! Ready?"

Basil's pressed his claws into Raoulino's tough scales.

"R-r-ready!" he called, in a shaky little voice.

"Here we go!"

Sam gave an encouraging chirp as Raoulino started to take off, flapping his wings very hard to make up for Basil's extra weight. For a few scary seconds it seemed as if they weren't going to get off the ground, but Raoulino clenched his teeth and beat his wings even harder, and a moment later they were in the air.

As Raoulino flapped his way higher into the sky, he heard a happy cheep, and saw Sam flying beside him. The sparrow gave him a quick, one-wing salute.

The breeze grew sharper and colder as they left the city and flew out over the harbor. Looking down, Raoulino saw the shadowy shapes of the ships, many, many more than he could count, all lined up in long, neat rows. In one of them, he hoped, the cobra was curled up safely, ready for his journey home.

The SS Thomas *is down there, too*, he thought, *ready to take me back to my island. I've got to get back as soon as I can. I don't want it to leave without me!*

He pumped his wings with all his might and soared out over the ocean.

The wind was strong now and smelled of salt and fish. Below him the sea moved restlessly, the choppy gray waves edged with white. Thunder growled again, and a chilly rain began to fall. Raoulino could feel Basil shivering on his back.

This is dangerous, he thought. *Basil got soaked before, and now he's getting cold and wet again. He's going to get sick!*

Quickly, Raoulino took ten deep breaths, making the flames in his chest burn red hot. So much heat flowed through his body that for a moment he felt as if his insides were melting. As he hoped, the extra heat warmed his friend, too, and in a few seconds Basil's shivering stopped.

They flew steadily on. The rain fell harder.

Suddenly, a flash of lightning lit up the cloudy sky, and Basil shouted, "Look! Down there! A ship!"

Raoulino peered through the darkness and saw a small boat making its way through the waves. He flew down to get a closer look. Lightning flickered again, and in its brightness Raoulino saw a red fishing boat with a picture of a silver swordfish painted on the boat's side.

"It's my boat! It's a Portland Fishing Company boat!" yelled Basil, wild with delight. "We did it!"

"Yes, we did!" Raoulino shouted, as he began flying down toward the boat. "Hold on! You're going home!"

All of a sudden, a huge bolt of lightning shot through the sky, followed by a crack of thunder so loud it sounded as if the sky had exploded. The rain started to fall in torrents. Blinded by the light flash and nearly dizzy from the thunder crash, Raoulino suddenly realized that he no longer felt Basil's weight on his back.

Basil was gone!

Raoulino's heart turned to ice. He swooped through the sky, desperately searching for his friend. At first he could see nothing but rain, clouds, and empty, gray ocean. Then, far below him, he glimpsed something fluttering in the air, just above the waves.

Could it be?

Yes!

It was Sam, clutching Basil by one leg, her wings beating furiously as she fought to keep him from dropping into the sea.

Raoulino shot through the air like a comet. Salt spray stung his eyes as he skimmed above the waves and caught Basil and Sam neatly on his back.

"Hold on!" he yelled. "I'm heading for the ship!"

Raoulino zoomed up, both his friends clinging tightly to his scales. Before long he saw the bright red ship plowing through the waves. He flew closer and studied it carefully. There was a pile of fishing nets on deck and no sailors in sight.

"Hang on," he cried. "We're landing!"

Fighting against the wind pushing at him from all sides, Raoulino flew straight toward the nets. As he curved his wings for the landing, a powerful gust caught him and blew him back up into the air.

"Don't worry," he called to his friends, who were desperately clinging to his back, "I can do it!"

He headed for the nets again. This time as he swooped down, he reached out with his front legs, dug his claws into the ropes, and hung on.

"Don't let go!" he shouted as his back legs touched down and he dug in with them, too. "We have to get out of the rain!"

Glancing around the deck, he saw the word LIFEBOAT painted on the wall. An arrow below it pointed to a little red boat strapped upside down and standing on four wooden blocks. With his friends on his back, Raoulino leaped to the deck, hurried to the boat, and crawled in underneath it. Looking up, he saw several wide, smooth planks where people could sit. He climbed up onto one and breathed a big sigh of relief.

"It's okay!" he said, raising his voice above the drumming sound of the rain. "We're safe!"

Panting and shivering, Basil and Sam slid off his back and collapsed.

Raoulino looked anxiously at his friends, who were sprawled on the plank with their eyes closed. Sam's feathers had kept her dry, but Basil was soaked and shivering. Careful not to start any more fires, Raoulino puffed out gusts of heated air until the space around them grew warm and cozy. Basil stopped shivering, opened his eyes, and sat up.

"Raoulino," he said, whispering so as not to wake Sam, who had fallen deeply asleep and was snoring gently, "you saved my life again. How can I ever thank you?"

"You don't have to thank me," Raoulino whispered back. "We're friends, and that's what friends do. After all, if you hadn't been so kind to me in the zoo and taught me how to read, we never would have escaped at all."

Basil nodded. "Yes," he said in a soft voice, "we're friends. And we'll always be friends, even if . . . if. . . ."

"Even if we never see each other again," Raoulino said sadly.

Basil nodded again, his eyes bright with tears.

As he thought about never seeing Basil again, tears rose in Raoulino's eyes, too.

They fell onto the plank, glimmered brightly for a moment, and turned into two sparkling green stones.

"R . . . Raoulino," stammered Basil, wide-eyed with astonishment, "what . . . what. . . .?"

"They're dragon tears," whispered Raoulino. "I saw some once before . . . in the zoo. . . ."

He reached out and touched the stones gently with his foot. Immediately, his heart grew lighter.

"We *will* see each other again," he said with a happy smile. "After all, Sam and I can fly, and we've all learned to travel. I can take a boat to Maine, and you and Sam can come to my island."

Basil looked up, sighing.

"Do you really think so? We'll be hundreds of miles away from each other."

"Think of what's happened already!" said Raoulino. "I turned out to be a dragon, we all escaped from the zoo, and we're on our way home. Would you ever have thought any of that was possible?"

"No," said Basil, slowly shaking his head. "I guess not."

"Other marvelous things will happen, too,"
Raoulino went on. He leaned forward and pushed
the stones toward Basil with his front leg.

"Take them," he said. "They're magic. They'll
keep you and Sam warm on the journey home."

"Really?" said Basil. He reached out and
touched the stone nearest him. Instantly, his face
brightened.

"You know," he said, sounding much more
cheerful, "you're right."

There was a loud clap of thunder. Sam opened
her eyes and sat up, chirping with surprise when
she saw the stones. She cheeped a question to

Basil, but before he could answer the roar of the engines grew much louder and the little boat picked up speed and began sailing faster and faster across the sea.

I'm getting farther and farther away from the harbor, thought Raoulino. *I have to go.*

"Basil," he said, his voice trembling, "I have to fly back now. I don't want the SS *Thomas* to leave without me!"

Basil stared at him for a moment.

"Yes, Raoulino," he whispered. "You're right."

Basil took a deep breath and raised one front leg in solemn salute.

"Good-bye, Raoulino, my dear friend," he said. "Good luck, until we see each other again."

Sam lifted her right wing and waved, chirping softly.

Raoulino took a last look at his friends. The lump in his throat had grown even larger, but he swallowed it bravely. He raised his tail and waved it jauntily at Basil and Sam.

"Good-bye for now," he said. "See you soon!"

Then he jumped down from the bench, crawled out from underneath the lifeboat, and flew over the ocean, alone.

Dawn was changing the sky from black to gray, but the storm still raged as Raoulino winged his way to the SS *Thomas*. He was tired and very hungry, but inside he was bubbling with happiness.

"Home!" he said to himself with every beat of his wings. "I'm going home!"

The city lights shone brighter and brighter as he neared the harbor. Looking down, he saw the long line of ships, tossing and straining against the heavy ropes that held them to the dock.

"Wow!" he said to himself. "There are so many of them. I hope the SS *Thomas* is still there!"

He flew closer and began reading the names painted in big letters on the sides of the ships: SS *Columbus* . . . SS *Van der Hoove* . . . SS *Santiago*. . . .

"It's got to be here," he said to himself anxiously. "It's just got to."

He kept on flying.

SS *Muscovy* . . . SS *Sussex*. . . . There it was . . . the SS *Thomas*! The very last ship in the line.

Raoulino whooped with joy and flew lower. Carefully scanning the ship, he saw a few people in yellow slickers on the front deck, but the back deck was deserted. And there were six big, upside down lifeboats where he could hide.

I did it! he thought to himself blissfully as he zoomed down, rounded his wings, and prepared to land. *I'm going home!*

All of a sudden, the ocean rolled, and the back deck rose sharply. Raoulino yelped as the railing smacked into his hind legs and flipped him into the sea. He struck the water hard and went under. Desperate with terror, he paddled his way up through the icy blackness and broke the surface, coughing and panting for breath.

The ocean heaved again.

A wall of water rose above Raoulino and then started to fall over him.

Heart hammering, beating his wings, and thrashing his tail with all his might, Raoulino burst out of the ocean and flew up into the sky. Drenched and shivering, he circled high above the SS *Thomas*, watching carefully as the ship pitched and tossed on the sea.

"I have to land while the ship is flat," he told himself. "Just after one end of the ship touches the water and before the other end starts to rise. It isn't going to be easy!"

He shivered again and took a deep breath to warm himself. His chest felt cold and empty.

Oh, no, he thought, his heart sinking, *my fire's gone out! I must have swallowed too much water!*

He flew another circle and tried to calm down.

"My flames will come back when I dry out," he told himself. "After all, I'm a dragon, and a dragon can't lose his fire that easily! Dragons are tough!"

He brushed the rainwater out of his eyes and

peered down at the ship. As he watched, the back end of the SS *Thomas* slanted up on a wave and hung there for a moment. Then the wave dropped, and for a few moments the big ship sat flat on the ocean.

Now! thought Raoulino.

He streaked down through the air and came in for his landing.

I've done it! he thought, his heart bursting with happiness.

An instant later, his feet skidded on the wet deck. Before he could even realize what was happening, Raoulino slid halfway across the ship and slammed headfirst into a rail.

Lights exploded behind his eyes.

Then everything went black.

When Raoulino woke up his head hurt, and he was weak and cold. He sat up slowly and looked around. The deck was wet, but it was not raining. Rays of sunlight shone down from a sky that was turning from gray to blue.

"Where am I?" he said to himself, staring in bewilderment at the deck, the rails, the huge, rolling gray sea. "This . . . this isn't the zoo. . . ."

He looked up and saw a tall smokestack. The words SS *Thomas* were painted on it in big black letters.

Suddenly he remembered.

I'm on the ship, he thought, a wave of joy washing over him. *The SS* Thomas! *I'm going home!*

He glanced around quickly. "I'd better try to

hide somewhere before somebody sees me," he said to himself.

Raoulino was so weak and tired that he could hardly stand. As he staggered up onto his front legs, he heard footsteps coming his way. Then a loud voice called, "Hey! Look at that!"

Oh no, thought Raoulino. *People!*

He looked up and saw two rough-looking sailors coming toward him.

I've got to get out of here, he thought.

He tried to flap his wings, but he was so weak he could hardly lift them. The sailors came closer and squatted down beside him.

"What do you think it is?" asked the one with the loud voice. He was a short man with a big belly and a bushy black beard.

"I dunno," said his friend, who was tall and thin and had a yellow moustache. "It looks like a kind of big green bat."

"I think it's sick," said the bushy bearded sailor. "See how it's shaking?"

"You stay here," said his friend. "I'm going to get Luis. He knows all about animals."

He hurried away. Raoulino lay on the deck, shivering.

"If they throw me overboard," he said to himself fiercely, "I'll spread my wings and float . . . I'm not going to give up now. . . . I'll NEVER give up . . . but oh, I'm so tired. . . ."

Raoulino heard footsteps coming toward him again. When he looked up, he could hardly believe his eyes. His heart leaped with happiness. The person walking next to the tall sailor was Raoulino's friend from the zoo!

When the little sailor saw Raoulino, he gasped, and his brown eyes grew enormous. He knelt down and gently scratched Raoulino under his chin.

"What happened to you, little fellow?" he asked. "And how did you *ever* get here?"

"What kind of animal is it, Luis?" the smaller sailor asked. "Do you know?"

"Oh, it's nothing special," Luis said quickly. "Just . . . um . . . just an ordinary green tree lizard. But he's looks kind of worn out. I'll take him down to my cabin and give him something to eat."

Luis picked Raoulino up and carried him down a narrow staircase to a small room with a round window in the wall. Locking the door behind them, Luis set Raoulino down on a soft pillow. Then he reached up, took a big glass bottle down from the shelf above the bed, and poured some green liquid into a bowl.

"Drink this, little guy," he said, putting the bowl down in front of Raoulino. "It will fix you up in no time."

Raoulino took a big gulp of the spicy green drink. As soon as he swallowed it, he felt a little "pop" in his chest. Then his stomach gurgled, and he burped out a lovely purple flame.

"Good!" said Luis, grinning at Raoulino, whose cheeks were flushed with embarrassment. "That's what Draconica Tea is *supposed* to do. The people on our island drink it because they like the taste, but it's very good for dragons. How do you feel now?"

Raoulino felt wonderful. His flames were burning again, sending strength and energy from the tip of his nose to the end of his tail and out to the edges of his wings. He leaped to his feet, spread his wings wide, and stretched his tail as far out as it would go.

Suddenly, the door rattled and a voice called, "Luis! Are you in there?"

"Uh-oh," said Luis.

He snatched Raoulino up, raced to the window, and pushed it open.

"You must go quickly, little fellow. If they see you and realize you are a dragon, they will never let you go!"

Luis leaned out of the window, still holding Raoulino in his hands.

"Our island is that way," he said, pointing straight ahead. "It is not very far. Good-bye, little fellow, and good luck!"

Raoulino looked back at him and waved his tail.

Luis smiled at him, gave him one last pat, and tossed him into the air.

14

The afternoon shadows were growing long when Raoulino caught his first glimpse of familiar green mountains rising from the sea.

My island, he thought, his flames exploding like fireworks in his chest. *I'm home!*

He pumped his wings even harder and sped across the glittering blue water. As the island came closer, Raoulino looked down and saw children playing on the beach, laughing and calling to one another as they frolicked at the water's edge.

"I'd better make sure no one sees *me*," he said to himself. "I don't want to end up in a cage again!"

He took a deep breath and soared higher into the sky. When the beach and the people were safely behind him, he came down lower and began searching for his home.

Our log was near a waterfall, he thought, *close to the edge of a pretty little lagoon. There was a big hibiscus bush in front of it, and two tall banana trees. . . .*

He looked down at the jungle-covered mountains below him, but there was no sign of a waterfall or a lagoon.

I must be on the wrong side of the island, he thought.

He zoomed over the tallest mountains and looked down again.

Yes!

There it was!

A silvery waterfall was flowing down the side of a smaller mountain, sending up a lovely, rainbow-colored spray as it splashed into a blue lagoon.

Raoulino's whole body trembled with joy.

"Home!" he said to himself. "I'm really, truly home!"

He plunged down from the sky, landed on top of a tall

flowering tree, and leaped lightly to the ground.

There, one end sticking out from behind the hibiscus bush, was his family's hollow log!

Raoulino was trembling so much he could hardly move. As he started toward the log, he heard the faint patter of footsteps, and a bright green lizard came out from behind the trunk of a banana tree. Her head drooped, and she moved slowly, as if she were old, or very, very sad.

Raoulino caught his breath.

Could it be?

Yes! Yes it was!

"Mother!" he shouted, dashing across the clearing. "Mother! I'm home!"

Raoulino's mother turned so pale she nearly disappeared.

"A dragon!" she said with a loud cry, her teeth chattering with terror. "It's . . . it's a dragon!"

She was shaking so badly, Raoulino was afraid she would faint.

I've changed so much she doesn't know who I am, Raoulino thought, *and she's frightened to death of me.*

"Please don't be afraid, Mother," he said, speaking as gently as he could. "It's me. It's Raoulino."

"Raoulino?" his mother said in a dazed-sounding voice. "You're . . . you're my son Raoulino?"

"Yes! Yes! It's really me," Raoulino said. "I got captured and taken to the zoo, and while I was there I grew into a dragon. But it's really me! Remember how you brought me home when I was a silvery green egg? Remember when I was little and I fell off the hibiscus bush and sprained my tail and you had to tie it up with liana vines? Remember when Dad brought you ginger flowers for your birthday, and I ate them for breakfast?"

"Yes," said his mother, her eyes wide with wonder. "I remember. But a dragon. . . ."

She lifted her head and looked deep into Raoulino's eyes. Raoulino looked back at her, his heart overflowing with love.

"Oh, Raoulino, it *is* you," she said, bursting into happy tears. "It's really you."

Her sobs were so loud that Raoulino's father and his four brothers and four sisters came running to see what was the matter.

"It's Raoulino!" Raoulino's mother cried as her children and her husband stood staring at him, their eyes nearly popping out of their heads. "He's a dragon! And he's come home!"

News of the little dragon's arrival spread quickly through the jungle. Parrots and butterflies flew down to see him, and little gray monkeys hung from the trees by their tails to see what all the commotion was about. Raoulino's aunts, uncles, and cousins came from all over the island, bringing gifts of nuts and berries and fruit to welcome him home. All afternoon Raoulino feasted with his family and took his brothers, his sisters, and his cousins for rides on his back. Over and over he told the story of his escape from the zoo.

A bright moon had risen in the sky by the time the last guest had left. As Raoulino and his family made their weary way to their log, they heard a sudden rustle of wings. An eerie green glow filled the air. They looked up, staring openmouthed as a dozen dragons skimmed over the treetops and landed in the clearing.

Raoulino's lizard family huddled together quaking with fear, but Raoulino felt only a great wave of joy.

There are *other dragons in the world*, he thought, staring at the dragons gleaming silvery green in the moonlight. *I'm* not *the only one! And oh! How beautiful they are!*

The largest dragon stepped forward, his black diamond eyes fixed on Raoulino.

"What is your name, little one?" he asked in a deep, rumbling voice.

"My name is Raoulino," Raoulino said.

"Raoulino," the dragon repeated thoughtfully. "And where do you come from?"

"I . . . uh . . . I came from the zoo," Raoulino

said. "I just got back today. But before that, I lived here, with my family."

"These lizards are your family?" the dragon asked, frowning.

"Yes," said Raoulino. "My mother found me and brought me home when I was just a silvery green egg. . . ."

"A silvery green egg!" the dragon roared, turning to Raoulino's mother. "Where, madam, did you find such an egg?"

"On the path near our home," said Raoulino's father, stepping in front of Raoulino's mother to protect her. "Some human children had been playing with it, rolling it and tossing it to one another. When they got tired of their game, they ran away and left it. If she had not taken it in, I do not think the egg would have survived."

Another dragon stepped forward. She was a little smaller than the first one, and her eyes were very bright.

"When . . . when did this happen? How . . . how long ago?"

"It was the year of the great storm," Raoulino's mother replied. She was still shaking, but she held her head high, and her voice was calm. "Only a moon or two before it happened."

"The year of the great storm!" the second dragon exclaimed, tears raining from her eyes. "Oh, Osric!" she said, turning to the leader. "He must be our son! He must be!"

"You must understand," she sobbed, turning back to Raoulino's mother. "We never thought we could lose him. I knew he was going to hatch soon, so I flew off to get some orchid petals and some bougainvillea leaves for him to eat. I wasn't afraid to leave him in the cave, for dragons' caves are so well hidden that we thought no stranger could find them. I had to fly to the other end of the island for the leaves, and when I came back, he was gone!"

The poor dragon broke down, sobbing so hard that she couldn't speak. Her tears struck the ground, making a little pile of rubies.

"There, there, Doriana," said Osric, patting her softly with his wing. "Try to calm yourself. Everything's all right now."

"Doriana gave the Dragon Alarm Roar right away," Osric continued, turning to Raoulino's parents, "and dragons came from everywhere to look for him. We found little human footprints in our cave, but we never found him. Until now."

"He must come back with us tonight," Doriana said, still sobbing. "We have so much to teach him . . . so much love to give. . . ."

Raoulino stared at the two dragons. There was a strange tearing pain in his chest, as if something were slowly splitting him in two.

"They're my parents," he said to himself. "I . . . I guess they're my *real* parents."

He looked at his lizard parents, who were watching him with anxious frowns on their faces.

But they're my real parents, too, he thought. *Oh! What am I going to do?*

He took a deep breath and sighed out a cloud of sickly looking green and yellow smoke. The dragons murmured softly among themselves. Osric shook his head.

"No, Doriana," he said. "We cannot take Raoulino from the only family he has ever known."

He took a step forward and gave Raoulino's lizard parents a deep bow.

"We will always be grateful to you," he said, "for saving our son's life and for giving him a happy home. We will go now, but may we have your permission to return tomorrow night so that Raoulino might get to know us a little better?"

Raoulino's lizard father bowed politely in return.

"You will be most welcome," he said. "Raoulino must get to know his dragon family. He is a dragon after all, though, he will always be our son as well as yours."

"Yes," said Doriana, smiling through her tears. "From now on Raoulino will have two families who love him!"

She came forward and kissed Raoulino tenderly on his cheek.

"Until tomorrow, Raoulino," Osric rumbled.

"Good night, Raoulino," the other dragons called softly.

"Good night," called Raoulino.

One by one the dragons spread their wings and flew into the night sky.

Raoulino watched them go, his heart glowing with happiness. Soon, he knew, he would be flying with them.

"Doriana is right," he said to himself. "Now I have *two* families that love me!"

He took a deep breath and blew out a cloud of glorious golden smoke. Then he followed his lizard family into their hollow log, curled up beside them, and went to sleep.

THE END